PETER RABBIT 2

TM

2

BASED ON THE
MAJOR NEW MOVIE

CONTENTS

Chapter One

"Cock-a-doodle-doo!" JW Rooster II crowed loudly on a glorious summer's day outside McGregor Manor. There is no better way to start a story than at a wedding – love, hope, and woodland animals . . . And this is where our story starts.

The beautiful wedding about to take place was filled with the finest of the finest – chairs, flowers, balloons. Johnny Town-mouse, a very well-dressed city mouse, was joined by three similarly well-dressed mice. The quartet began to sing.

The groom, a man named Thomas McGregor, waited at the altar for his bride-to-be. He was flanked not by best men, but two small rabbits. Peter was a determined and clever bunny with a cheeky grin and a knack for getting into trouble. His cousin Benjamin was wise, supportive, and looked for all the world as if his ears had been stuck on upside down.

Peter and Benjamin, of course, were not the only animals in attendance. The bride, Bea, was a dear friend to a host of countryside creatures. Her guest list included ducks, badgers, foxes, and a

7

very prickly hedgehog called Mrs. Tiggy-winkle. At this moment all of these animals were trying to pin tiny buttonhole bouquets onto their tiny jackets.

Bea appeared, dressed in a heavenly white wedding dress. She blushed with happiness, then started to make her way down the aisle toward Thomas. Three delightful rabbits skipped in front of her, scattering rose petals along the path. Flopsy, Mopsy, and Cotton-tail were Peter's triplet sisters.

"She's so beautiful," Mopsy whispered breathlessly.

Flopsy concentrated hard, repeating over and over, "Not going to cry. Not going to cry."

The third bunny, Cotton-tail, shot them a look – softies. She liked to think of herself as tougher than her sisters. She heard more snuffling behind and turned to see Pigling Bland following in their wake, snorting up the rose petals.

"Beat it, Pig," she told him.

Pigling Bland closed his mouth abruptly, swallowed, and tried to look innocent.

Bea finally made it to the altar and kissed her father. Her father shook Thomas's hand as the officiant stepped to the front.

"Welcome, friends, large and small, two-legged and four," she said, smiling at the guests as Thomas patted Peter on the head and Peter smiled. "We are gathered here today to join Bea and Thomas in holy matrimony."

Benjamin whispered to Peter. "You're taking this so well," he said. When Thomas McGregor had first arrived in Windermere, things had got off to a very shaky start. Thomas's great-uncle, the first Mr. McGregor, had lived next door to Bea for years. The old grump absolutely hated the rabbits who stole vegetables from his garden. Every waking moment was spent guarding his beans, carrots, and lettuces. Then, on one terrible day, Mr. McGregor had managed to catch Peter's father and bake him in a pie. Peter had never forgiven him. It was understandable therefore, why Peter and the young Mr. McGregor had not seen eye to eye at first. But things were different now. Peter was a changed rabbit.

"He's a good man," Peter nodded, gazing up at the couple beside him. "Makes her happy."

". . . and also a special day for their family, the beloved rabbits," continued the vicar. "Welcoming a new parent – a father, if you will."

Peter frowned. "Father?"

Suddenly and without warning the rabbit lunged at Thomas. Flopsy and Mopsy began tackling a violinist, chairs went flying, and the flower arch was knocked to the floor. Pandemonium broke out. Pigling Bland took a whopping bite out of the wedding cake. Peter kicked the groom in the tummy, sending him reeling into a row of large balloons. Thomas struggled to escape from the tangled strings, but it was hopeless and he began to float away!

Poor Bea looked up as her soon-to-be husband floated into orbit. Thinking fast, she sprinted toward another cluster of balloons, held on tight, and took off after him. Peter grabbed Mrs. Tiggy-winkle and leaped for Bea's feet.

Bea shot up toward Thomas, who lunged at her. She caught him in midair with the ease of a trained trapeze artist. She gave a nod to Peter, still dangling below. The rabbit lifted up Mrs. Tiggy-winkle, who started to fire quills at the balloons.

Pop! Pop! Pop!

The happy couple fell out of the sky like rocks. In a superhero-style move, Peter flew in front of them, opening up his jacket like a flying squirrel. He touched down on the ground, and caught Bea and Thomas safely in his arms, just as fireworks began to light up the sky . . .

Except that didn't happen. This is what Peter of the last tale would have done. The Peter of this tale had learned from his mistakes.

Benjamin poked his cousin in the ribs. "Peter! The ring. The ring!"

"Right," said the rabbit. "Sorry."

Peter reached into the pocket of his jacket for the wedding band, but it wasn't there. He tried the other pocket. Again, nothing. Everyone stared as he frantically searched for the vital piece of jewelry. A woman coughed.

"I knew he couldn't be trusted," said Thomas.

But then, and to his greatest relief, Peter found the ring and handed it to Mr. McGregor. Thomas nuzzled the rabbit affectionately, in an almost fatherly manner, then carefully slipped the wedding band on Bea's finger.

"You may now kiss the groom," the officiant said. And Bea did. Everyone cheered except Cotton-tail, who bawled. Flopsy and Mopsy gave her a look – softy!

"I have something in my eye," she protested, plucking out a piece of lint. "And I'm crying."

Bea bent down to hug Peter, and the couple walked down the aisle together hand in hand, as Johnny Town-mouse and the quartet sang. It was such a joyful moment that no one noticed or even cared that Pigling Bland was greedily scoffing up the confetti-rice as soon as people threw it over the newlyweds.

So Peter didn't ruin the wedding. Bea and Mr. McGregor were married and headed off on their honeymoon in their car, a **JUST MARRIED** banner dangling from the bumper. The guests – both human and animal – waved them goodbye. Things couldn't have been more peaceful in Windermere, until some time later ...

Chapter Two

One day in his toyshop, Thomas was busy demonstrating a new doll to a little boy.

"You just take the dummy out . . . ," he explained, pulling it out of the doll's mouth. Right on cue, the toy began to cry. When Thomas put the dummy back in again, the doll went quiet. "Now you try."

Thomas passed the doll to the little boy, then headed over to the cash register and Bea.

"Beautiful sound, that," he said, as the boy made the doll cry all over again. "A family."

"We're a family." Bea smiled and gestured across the store toward Peter, Benjamin, Flopsy, Mopsy, and Cotton-tail.

"Yes, we are blessed," Thomas agreed. "But there's also that old-fashioned definition of a family. You know, when *humans* become parents to other *humans*."

Before Bea could reply, a boy in the shop called out.

"Dad! It's Peter Rabbit from the book!"

The little boy grabbed his father's hand and pointed to Peter. There in the center of the shop was a display made up of dozens of books.

Bea had been published!

"I hate that I'm the face of this," said Peter. "It's the story of all of us."

The other bunnies rolled their eyes.

The boy continued to tell his father all about the story. "Peter doesn't have a dad. He got put in a pie. That's why he's so naughty ..." Peter's whole body sagged – why did everybody think he was naughty? Suddenly, the boy noticed the others. "And there's his sisters – Flopsy, Mopsy, and Cotton-tail!"

The overexcited kid pointed at the rabbits but confused Flopsy and Mopsy.

"I'm Flopsy," said Flopsy.

"And *I'm* Mopsy," piped up her sister. "Why does everyone do that? We don't look alike at all."

"At least you got a mention," sighed Benjamin. Cotton-tail thoughtfully stomped on his foot so that he yelped.

"And Benjamin!" cried the boy.

Benjamin was rather touched. "Thank you."

A woman picked up one of the books and made her way to the cash register, where there was a sign declaring **30% DONATED TO LAND PRESERVATION**.

"Are you the author?" asked the lady.

"It's really the rabbits' story," Bea said. "I just wrote it down. My husband is the publisher."

"I wouldn't say *publisher*," Thomas McGregor chipped in, "I just turned our dining room into a workshop, do all the typesetting, artisanal lithography with a five-color palette for the illustrations, except for ones of the garden that call for more green . . ."

"Shh!" Bea shushed. "Don't reveal your secrets, honey. Keep it a mystery."

"Well, it's wonderful," the woman replied. "You paint the rabbits with such love."

"They're my family." Bea smiled, glancing at Thomas and the rabbits. "It comes naturally. And thanks for your contribution. It goes right to preserving their land."

Just then, the postman knocked on the window as he placed the mail in the letterbox. Peter scurried outside, where there was a big sign showing a picture of Peter from the book cover. As Peter jumped up to fetch the mail, two girl rabbits walked past.

"Are you Peter?" one giggled.

Peter tried to be smooth. "That depends who's asking."

"She's asking," said the second bunny. "She just asked you."

"Then I guess I owe you an answer," Peter replied, leaning against the sign. It began to wobble alarmingly, but Peter grabbed it and righted it. He leaned against it again. The girls laughed.

"You're funny," they said.

"Among other things," he replied just as the board collapsed under his weight. With an unfortunate crack, the window began to break, and Peter hit the pavement. Peter tried to pose smoothly on the floor as Thomas's furious face appeared in the shop window.

"Peter!"

"So it *is* you!" the first girl squealed.

Later that day, Thomas was still taping up the broken window. Peter looked on sheepishly.

"I'm sure it was just an accident," Bea said, kneeling down to comfort him.

"It wasn't an accident," insisted Thomas. "It's what he does. He never behaves."

"Don't listen to him," Bea whispered to Peter. "He loves you."

"He *doesn't* listen to me. That's the problem!" Thomas replied.

Bea frowned at her husband. She didn't want him to speak that way about Peter, especially not in front of him! Thomas couldn't see what the problem was in speaking his mind. Rabbits couldn't understand human speech – everyone knew that!

It didn't take long, however, to see that Bea wasn't going to give in. Thomas sighed. "But of course I love you," he said in a stilted voice to Peter. "Like an adult man loves a teenage rabbit."

Peter slunk back to join the others.

"I didn't mean to," Peter repeated.

Benjamin, who always understood, put a reassuring arm round his cousin.

Bea continued to sort the mail. As she leafed through the letters, she came across a fancy envelope addressed to her.

"What's this? Basil-Jones Publishing?"

Thomas's eyes lit up. Before he came to Windermere he had worked in the toy department at Harrods in London. They had carried a whole section of Basil-Jones books at the famous department store. "That was the last display I arranged before I resigned."

"You mean fired and physically removed from the store," Bea reminded him as she read on.

"Potato, *potahto*," replied Thomas.

"Potato, psychotic breakdown," said Bea.

"But I'm all better now, right?" her husband asked, fishing for a compliment.

Bea opened the envelope and gasped as she read the letter. "It's from Nigel Basil-Jones himself. He wants to publish my book! Get it in every bookstore, promote it, put it in different languages ..."

"That's incredible!" cried Thomas.

Bea read on. "He wants us to come to Gloucester. You too. Wants to meet 'the genius' who used a five-color palette for the illustrations."

"Except for the garden ones that called for more green," corrected Thomas. "But yes! This is it, Bea! It's happening."

Bea and Thomas pulled each other into a tight hug and began to jump up and down, knocking a display of dolls over as they bounded around the shop.

This mishap did not go unnoticed by Peter. "Oh sure, *he* makes a mistake and no one yells at him," he muttered, watching the newlyweds embrace. "And he even gets a kiss. Which is disgusting, so it's fine, I guess."

When the family drove home that evening, Bea could talk of nothing but the possibility that her *Peter Rabbit* book was going to be published.

"Should I call him? Should I write to him?" she gushed. "Maybe just a casual drop-by: 'Oh hello, Nigel Basil-Jones, just happened to be in the Publishing District?' No, that's too needy. I know!

18

I'll completely ignore him! Then he'll *know* I mean business."

Thomas beamed. "I love seeing you this excited, and a bit unhinged . . ."

"You're running low," Bea said, glancing at the fuel gauge.

"I meant to fill it today," Thomas said, "but I forgot my work gloves, and when my hands smell like petrol I sneeze."

Bea tried not to grin.

"I'm proud of you," said Thomas. "You finally found your voice; it deserves to be heard."

"I love you, Mr. McGregor." Bea smiled.

Thomas began to reply, "And I love you, Mrs. McG–" but before he could complete the sentence, Bea interrupted him.

"Bup-bup-bup!"

Thomas quickly began his memorized line. "Taking my last name would perpetuate the patriarchy."

"Plus, it sounds like a brand of biscuits," Bea reminded him.

The Land Rover crunched along the lane toward a pear tree. Peter pounded on the window. He and the other rabbits had been riding together in the back. As soon as they got close to the tree, the animals scurried up onto the roof.

"Ready?" cried Bea. At just the right moment, she pushed the accelerator pedal to the floor and the Land Rover plunged forward, sending the rabbits flying high up into the air. With their paws outstretched, the bunnies expertly plucked several pears from the branches of the fruit tree before falling back into the truckbed in a big, fluffy pile, all on top of Benjamin.

"Your foot's in my mouth, Flopsy," Benjamin spluttered.

"That's my foot!" Mopsy cried indignantly. "We're different! And from now on, I'm going to make sure everyone knows!"

"Me too," Flopsy agreed.

"Starting now!" the rabbits said in unison.

They tried again.

"Now!" Again they spoke at exactly the same time.

"Now!" And again . . .

"Ugh . . . ," they moaned in unison. "This is going to be tough."

Chapter Three

As soon as the Land Rover pulled into the drive of McGregor Manor, Peter and the rabbits bounded off toward the vegetable garden. When it had belonged to the Old Mr. McGregor, the place had been out-of-bounds in a big way. The gate was padlocked, and the animals knew that they entered at their own peril. Mr McGregor regularly patrolled the borders and hedgerows with a hoe, threatening to smack it down on any creature bold enough to even peep at his precious harvest. Now, however, it was a very different story. Not only were there no patrols, there was no gate. The garden was a bunny's paradise – stocked to the tip-top with row upon row of sweet strawberries, ripe radishes, and crunchy carrots.

"Let's get some stuff for dinner!" Peter yelled, running toward the lettuces.

"Ooh, yeah," agreed Benjamin. "I was thinking of making a harvest consommé with a . . ."

Peter and the triplets had no intention of waiting for all this delicious produce to be chopped, sliced, and sautéed, then served up in a dish.

"Or we could just shove it down our throats," Peter said to his cousin, cramming handfuls of vegetables into his open mouth.

Thomas McGregor had also decided to enjoy the garden that evening. He wasn't there to eat, however; he had come to inspect. He stood in the center of a flawless square plot, silently counting up shiny red fruit. His prized tomatoes.

"They're all still here," he said at last. Thomas's tomatoes were his pride and joy. They looked so succulent and juicy and he could never quite trust that the rabbits – particularly Peter – would be able to keep their paws off them.

"Of course they are," Bea said, wandering along behind him. "They know how much they mean to you."

Thomas crouched down and swept a long finger through the soil at the base of his biggest plant. He brought it to his mouth and tasted.

"Too moist," he pronounced seriously. "I need the hairdryer."

He was just about to head into the house to fetch one when Bea, who had been staring at the ruby jewels, reached out to pluck one off its vine.

Thomas didn't even need to look back.

"Bup-bup-bup!" he called over his shoulder, stopping her in her tracks.

Bea groaned, then released the tomato and followed Thomas inside.

Mrs. Tiggy-winkle watched the pair go. "That city man sure loves his tomatoes," she declared.

"Oh, because he's from the city he can't be a farmer?" Pigling Bland retorted sniffily. "Can't we determine our own identity? I'm a pig, does that mean I must roll around in the mud and overeat?"

Mrs. Tiggy-winkle pointed at a fresh compost heap in the corner. "Check out that pile of garbage."

"WHERE?"

Pigling leaped on to the heap, then rolled around in the stinky mulch, chomping down as many scraps as possible.

"I did this by choice," he snorted, pretty sure he had maintained the higher ground.

After their al fresco feast, the rabbits hopped into the house with Bea. The dining room was no longer a place to eat – it had become a busy printing workshop. Stacks of paper, letter blocks, and ink bottles covered every surface. This was where Thomas turned Bea's work into beautiful, brilliant color books.

"I can't believe this might actually turn into

something big," marveled Bea, picking up an illustration. She shook her head, then turned to leave, accidentally knocking the picture to the floor. Peter scampered over to take a look at it.

The picture was a portrait that Bea had painted of Peter and his dad. As he stared at his familiar face, a stream of vivid memories crowded into his head.

His father tossing vegetables over the garden wall for Peter to catch on the other side.

The time his dad taught him exactly the right way to sneak under the gate without snagging his jacket.

Frantic runs up and down the rows of vegetables, side by side with his dad as an indignant Old Mr. McGregor chased vainly after them.

His mother's smiling face as Peter and his dad triumphantly brought armfuls of food home to the family.

Too soon the memories faded and vanished. Peter was left alone, staring forlornly at paint on paper.

"Miss you, Pops," he murmured. "No one gets me the way you did."

Suddenly, a telephone rang and Thomas appeared to snap the bunny out of his reverie.

"I'll get it!" he bellowed, striding into the room. Thomas glanced down and saw Peter holding the illustration. Without wondering or asking why he might be looking at it, Thomas yanked the sheet out of the little rabbit's paws

"You know not to touch this!" he tutted. "Honestly."

Bea's voice echoed out across the hall. "It might be the publisher!"

Thomas straightened up, put the illustration of Peter and his dad back on the table, then stalked out in pursuit of the still-jangling phone.

Alone again, Peter heard a rustling noise outside. He crossed to the window and looked out. Tommy Brock the badger was in the garden, snuffling about in the tomato patch! Uh-oh.

Quick as a flash Peter disappeared outside. He bounded as fast as his legs would carry him toward the hungry badger, just in time to see Tommy lift a shining tomato to his mouth.

"No, Tommy!" puffed Peter, snatching the contraband away. "Those are Mr. McGregor's!"

"Whah?" Tommy was outraged . . . and ravenous. "B-b-but you used to steal from him all the time."

Peter stayed firm. "We share the garden now."

"B-b-because he married the lady, you do what he says now?" spluttered Tommy.

"No, not because of that," snapped Peter, feeling rather irritable. "Well, kind of because of that. Just don't touch the tomatoes, badger!"

Tommy Brock had seen a few things in his time, but this was hard to swallow. A pact between a man and a rabbit? What was the world coming to? He took one last lunge at the fruit, before Peter shooed him away.

Once he was certain that the badger had gone elsewhere for his supper, Peter tried to repair the damage to Thomas's precious crop. He tenderly picked weeds from the ground and smoothed out the crumpled leaves.

While Peter worked in the tomato patch, Bea had finally located the telephone. She chatted to the publisher, Nigel, trying her hardest not to sound too excited. When he suggested a visit to his office, she shot a thrilled look to Thomas, who was sitting beside her.

"The eleven-fifteen train to Gloucester," she repeated breathlessly. "We'd love to bring the rabbits. It would be a fun adventure."

Thomas was listening intently, until he gazed out of the window and spotted Peter! That naughty rabbit sat in the middle of his tomato patch, putting his paws all over the vines.

Thomas hammered angrily on the window.

Bang! Bang! Bang!

How dare Peter be so willfully disobedient? He had the run of the entire garden. Only the tomatoes were sacred. His prized tomatoes. His pride and joy.

Peter gestured frantically at Thomas. He wanted to show him that he had been trying to save, not steal the tomatoes. But the more he waved, the more Thomas scowled. He did not believe him.

The very instant that Bea hung up the phone, Thomas wrenched open the window and roared at the bunny, "Leave my tomatoes alone! You have everything else!"

Peter's shoulders slumped. He set the lone tomato that Tommy had tried to eat down at the foot of its vine, then silently lolloped away.

"See?" Thomas McGregor told his wife in angry exasperation. "I've told him a million times. He doesn't listen."

"Go easy," urged Bea, pecking Thomas on the cheek. "He's still getting used to the idea that you're here to stay."

Chapter Four

Soon Bea, Thomas, and the bunnies took the train to Gloucester. They were heading for the publisher's office. The group settled into a large, lavish compartment. There were gift baskets full of vegetables for the rabbits and others full of treats for Bea and Thomas. Bea read the note attached to a beautifully produced copy of her book.

Enjoy the journey. It's just the beginning.
Nigel

Bea frowned. "A bit presumptuous."

Thomas turned the card over and read the back.

Forgive me for being presumptuous.

The rabbits were perched on a seat across the carriage making the most of the new experience. Flopsy and Mopsy were trying to watch the view from the window, their heads flying back and forth furiously as the scenery flashed past.

"As someone who's been on a train before – a few pointers," said Benjamin. "Don't stare at the scenery rushing by – look at a fixed point on the horizon."

"I'm feeling sick," gasped Flopsy, her head swiveling frantically.

"No, *I'm* feeling sick," insisted Mopsy.

And with that, both sisters fell to the floor.

"You OK, sweeties?" asked Bea, helping the rabbits back onto the seat. The pair went straight back to trying to keep up with the flickering view, heads turning to and fro, to and fro. Very quickly, they both collapsed again in a dizzy heap.

Bea sat down beside Thomas. He had picked up a tourist brochure about a farmers' market in Gloucester. The flyer proclaimed that anyone was free to sell as long as their produce was of the finest quality.

Thomas was pondering this so deeply, he didn't notice Cotton-tail nibbling colorful jelly beans from the adults' gift basket.

"Has anyone tried one of these magic beans?" she said loudly. "They'll change your life." The bunny backflipped off the table, landing perfectly. "They look like beans, but they taste like rainbows and laughter and Saturday mornings!"

"How many of those have you had?" asked Peter.

"I don't know. I don't know. I don't know. I don't know. I don't know. I don't know. Is it hot in here? I'm cold. Stop yelling at me!"

Oh dear. The sugar was hitting hard. Peter and Cotton-tail stared at each other for a moment, then the sister rushed out of the compartment

29

and appeared *outside* the window! She clung on with all her fingers and toes.

"I'm going to live forever!" she screamed joyfully through the glass.

The compartment was plunged into darkness as the train raced through a tunnel. As they emerged Peter stared at the window. There was no Cotton-tail. THWACK! She had flung herself back onto the window.

"Told you!"

A couple of hours later, everyone was sitting in the publisher's office.

"There they are!" Nigel Basil-Jones gushed. "Bea. You're even more lovely than your jacket portrait." The publisher kissed her hand, then reached out to her husband. "And Thomas. Even handsomer than I'd imagined!" At last he turned to the rabbits. "And the stars themselves. They must be tuckered."

Nigel Basil-Jones was very handsome and charming. His office was huge and elegantly decorated – every shelf was lined with best-selling books and merchandise. It was all rather impressive.

Nigel showed the rabbits to an area set out just

for their comfort. There were squashy pillows and a big empty bowl. An assistant instantly appeared with two jugs of water. "Sparkling and still," she announced as the bunnies scampered over.

"I want sparkling," said Flopsy. "What's sparkling?"

"It must glow in the dark," decided Mopsy.

Nigel Basil-Jones wasted no time in getting down to business. "I'm so glad you came," he said. "I'm sure I'm one of many beating down your door begging to publish your next book."

"So many," said Bea, desperate to sound professional, "we had to get a new door. Beaten right off its hinges."

"If you'll allow me to gush, your book is absolutely exquisite. A triumph."

Bea smiled. "I'll allow you."

"'What better gift than the love of a rabbit,'" Basil-Jones quoted.

Bea tried not to look too confused.

"Charles Dickens," Nigel explained. "Well, he said 'a cat,' but you obviously knew that."

"Of course!" Bea lied. "I love Dickens. Know every word he's written."

Thomas gawped at his wife. "You do?"

Basil-Jones chuckled, then gave Thomas a hearty pat on the back.

"Strong," he remarked. "What do you do – box?"

It was Thomas's turn to spin a tale now.

"Oh, sure," he bragged, "among other things. Weights, metal bars, big balls of sand, protein ointment . . ."

Bea shot him a look.

"We should get in the ring sometime," Basil-Jones said. "Now, I'd like to walk you through our strategy."

He brought them toward a table and outlined his plan. "I want to start by printing five thousand copies of your book. And I assume you want to write a second?"

"I haven't really thought about it," Bea pretended, "but . . . I guess I do have a brief framework for a twenty-three-book series featuring a hundred and nine characters based on the animals in my life, creating an interwoven narrative about morality, nature, and family, set in the fields and towns around our farm."

She spotted Thomas's incredulous look. "I had a lot of time on my hands before I met you," she explained.

"Fantastic," Basil-Jones enthused. "Because it's in your next book that we see huge potential."

Nigel gestured to his assistant, who wordlessly handed him a stack of posters.

32

On the other side of the room, Flopsy plucked up the courage to take a sip of the sparkling water.

"Bleuch!" she groaned, crinkling her nose and cleaning her tongue with her paws. "It's like drinking sand."

"I like it. It's delicious," Mopsy exclaimed.

"You're just saying that to be different."

"Am not."

"Drink the whole thing, then," Flopsy dared her.

Mopsy immediately sucked down the water, her face a picture of pain. "It's . . . amazing," she spluttered, crying and spitting at the same time.

Basil-Jones's assistant revealed a poster of Bea's painting, as Nigel continued. "We've done some research on your book. People liked the story and setting, but what they really loved were the rabbits."

Peter Rabbit pricked up his ears, shooting the others a congratulatory wink.

"So," Basil-Jones continued, "with the second book we'd really like to emphasize their individuality."

He nodded to the aide, who revealed Benjamin's portrait, deep in thought, his hand on his chin.

"Benjamin," Basil-Jones declared. "The Wise One."

"It's true." Peter nodded, ear-fiving his cousin. "You are smart."

The next painting was unveiled. It showed Cotton-tail leaping through the air.

"Cotton-tail. The Firecracker."

Again Peter laughed. "That is who you are. This guy is good."

The aide revealed a third painting. Flopsy and Mopsy grinned from it, arms defiantly crossed.

"Flopsy and Mopsy," declared Basil-Jones. "The Dynamic Duo."

Peter approved. "Nailed it! Baboom!"

"And finally, Peter."

Peter Rabbit looked up in mock-surprise. "What?" he asked innocently. "I get one? This is crazy!"

"We have two options for him," said Basil-Jones.

"I get two! Is this really happening? I mean . . . what!" laughed Peter. He puffed his chest, certain the strapline would be something like: HERO.

"The Mischief-Maker."

Peter shrugged. This was not exactly what he'd hoped for.

"Or . . . ," Basil-Jones continued.

Peter looked to the others confidently.

The second poster was uncovered. Peter scowled sullenly from the canvas.

Basil-Jones's voice rang out. "The Bad Seed."

Chapter Five

At first there was only stunned silence. Peter's whole body shrank. Everyone else looked shocked, apart from ...

"*That's* the one," Thomas blurted out. "Nailed it."

Nigel Basil-Jones was delighted. "It's our favorite, too," he said, nodding excitedly. "Really speaks to his character."

Bea seemed less sure. "'Bad seed' seems a little harsh."

But Basil-Jones was once again on a roll.

"He really is, you know," the publisher boomed, warming to his theme. "He nearly broke you two up and destroyed his own family. Electrocutions, rake attacks ..."

"He's a little mischievous," Bea conceded, "but he doesn't mean anything by it."

"I did catch him stealing one of my tomatoes yesterday," Thomas remarked.

"I also imagine his voice would be quite irritating," said Basil-Jones.

This last insult was too much for Peter. "Whaaat?" he gasped. "Come on! I mean!"

Sadly no one was listening anymore.

Nigel Basil-Jones gestured to his aide and led the group outside.

"I have something else to show you."

Nigel took Bea and Thomas by the arm, positioning them carefully in just the right place on the pavement below. Bea gazed up to a giant billboard, draped in fabric.

Basil-Jones flashed his widest smile.

"Here's how much we want to do this with you," he told Bea, pulling on a cord beside him. The fabric swept back, revealing the enormous billboard.

COMING SOON: A NEW BOOK BY THE AUTHOR OF PETER RABBIT!

The poster featured a gigantic painting of the rabbits. Each creature stood at least ten feet tall. They looked like a band of long-eared super-heroes ... except for Peter. The billboard version of Peter stood apart from the other rabbits, arms folded, face curled in a sneer of disdain.

There was another stunned silence.

"Whoa," gasped Thomas.

"That's incredible!" whispered Bea.

"My ears are gigantic!" Benjamin cried.

Thomas stood back to appraise the billboard

properly. "Peter really looks like a villain," he concluded at last.

"Every story needs one," said Basil-Jones, clearly proud of his handiwork.

Peter looked pleadingly at Bea. She always, always had his back, and yet her expression now appeared to be one of excitement.

Suddenly, she noticed a small, smiling face peeking into the scene at the corner of the billboard.

"Is that me in the corner?" she asked, secretly delighted, but trying to be modest.

"Oh no," replied Basil-Jones. "That's Mrs. Tiggy-winkle. We think she's a real breakout."

"Aah," said Bea, peering closer and seeing that it was indeed the face of her favorite hedgehog. "Well, I love it. It's terrific."

Thomas put his arm round Bea, then drew in the rabbits for a family group hug. No one picked up on Peter's mood. Right now he looked as if he'd just taken a jab to the stomach.

"I'm going to take a walk," he whispered to the others.

No one answered.

"So I'm going to go grab some air," he said again. Nothing.

"You're good here? OK," he piped up. "What?

Did you say something?"

No one was saying anything – at least, not to him.

"No?" he continued, his voice trailing away into a murmur. "OK, enjoy the billboard . . ."

And, unnoticed by Basil-Jones, his assistant, or any other member of the McGregor family, the real, live Peter Rabbit loped sadly away.

Peter had never been to Gloucester before. He wandered down side streets, ambled down alleys, and hopped along lanes. There were hardly any people in the shadows behind the hustle and bustle of the high street, although he did pass a familiar and very talented busking quartet. Johnny Town-mouse's sorrowful crooning perfectly matched Peter's mood. He turned another corner where the buildings were lower and found that when he looked up, he could still see the billboard. It seemed to loom inescapably over him at every corner.

Peter turned his back on the picture. This new street was busier, peppered with colorful market stalls with produce piled high in tall pyramids. Peter spied an older rabbit standing right beside a fruit vendor.

As Peter gawped, the rabbit expertly kicked the base of the display, causing a lone peach to roll off the top of the pyramid and fall straight into his outstretched paws.

The rabbit smirked then turned away. As he did, he caught Peter's eye. "What are you looking at, son?" he growled.

Peter started. This rabbit was clearly from the city streets. He was gruff, rough, and tough.

The rabbit took a few steps toward Peter. "You gonna turn me in?" he demanded to know. "You some kind of goody-goody?"

Peter's eyes flicked up at the display and then back at the stranger. Quick as a fiddle, he kicked the bottom of the display and dislodged a ripe, round peach, sending it toppling directly down into his waiting paws.

"I'm no goody-goody," Peter replied.

But the rabbit didn't react quite as Peter had expected.

With a cry of, "Look out!" he yanked Peter by the arm, just in time to avoid the business end of a cricket bat.

Whack! The bat smashed down on the pavement.

Peter peered up to see an angry shopkeeper hauling the bat back above his shoulder, ready to take another swing.

"Get out of here, rats!" he yelled, eyeing them both with malice.

Peter ran before the shopkeeper could bring the cricket bat crashing down again.

The older rabbit ran ahead, guiding Peter along with him. Suddenly, the stranger took an enormous spring and leaped into a letterbox.

Peter didn't twitch. He went right after him.

Chapter Six

It was dark inside the letterbox. The only sound came from Peter. The older rabbit climbed up the stack of letters and peeked through the slot. The shopkeeper ran by, hot on the tail of the pair of . . . rats.

"We'll be fine in a minute," he reassured Peter, peeling a stamp from a letter and licking it. "Have a sugar square."

Peter took another square of paper and licked it. Wow! It tasted great!

"I thought these were just tiny drawings of old ladies in hats," he exclaimed, taking another lick.

The older rabbit cocked his head, regarding Peter with interest. "You look just like an old friend of mine from the country," he said. "Had a jacket like yours."

Peter looked down at his faded blue coat. He gently felt the smooth lapel. "It was my dad's."

The old rabbit sat up straight.

"We used to steal from this old farmer together," he said with a grin. "McGillicuddy ... McDougal ...?"

"McGregor?" Peter finished.

"Yes!" the older rabbit's ears pricked up. "Wait a

minute . . . Your pops, is he, no longer with us? In that great pie in the sky?"

Peter was astonished. "How do you know that?"

"He was my best mate," replied the rabbit. "Are you . . . Peter?"

"Yes," Peter replied simply.

"Well" – the old rabbit grinned – "you're the spitting image of your old man. My name's Barnabas."

Peter was shocked. "Hi," he ventured.

Suddenly, there was a dull clunk and the letter-box was suddenly flooded with light. The collection door had been unlocked! A landslide of bills, cards, and packages began to shift down toward the open door.

"Uh-oh." Barnabas frowned. "Sugar man's here."

Somehow the pair managed to scramble past the postman and his gaping sack. Mail flew left and right as the pair bounded toward the exit. They were fast, but not fast enough to entirely avoid being sprayed by a can in the postman's hand.

The spray stung Peter's eyes. "What was that?" he said, blinking.

"Pepper spray," Barnabas explained. "It's what they spray on peppers to make 'em spicy."

The pair hopped along side by side until . . . WHOMP! The shopkeeper was back.

Without a moment's hesitation, Barnabas jumped up onto a row of recycling bins. Peter just had time to note that each was clearly labeled – PAPER, PLASTIC, GLASS, and METAL – before he, too, disappeared inside.

But while the letterbox had offered temporary shelter, the bunnies were rapidly running out of luck. The shopkeeper had seen Barnabas popping his head out of the PAPER bin.

"I'll get *you* sorted," he cried, whacking his broom down on the lid with all his might.

Peter popped his head out of the METAL bin, unable to resist checking on Barnabas ...

CLANG!

The broom narrowly missed him. There followed a crazy and dangerous game that saw the rabbits popping their heads out of bins while the shop-keeper tried to hit them before they disappeared and resurfaced somewhere else.

WHACK! BOOM! BANG!

Again and again the furious shopkeeper brought his broom down on the lids, but now they knew the rules, the rabbits were much too quick. After a little while, the pair even found time to rearrange some of the wrongly sorted garbage.

"It's not that hard, people!" shouted Peter as Barnabas plucked a soda can out of the

PAPER bin and threw it to Peter to dispense in METAL.

The rabbits finally escaped. The pair flew out of the recycling and through the man's legs, before dashing away down the street.

Peter skidded around a corner, but Barnabas was just a little too slow. Suddenly, the postman stepped out onto the pavement. The postman shot out a hand and grabbed Barnabas by the ears.

Peter slipped around the corner and watched as the shopkeeper appeared at the postman's side. The two men were deep in discussion, while poor Barnabas swung helplessly between them.

There was no time to think. Peter charged at the postman, his eyes fixed on the can of pepper spray tucked under his belt. Peter leaped up, grabbed the can, and sprayed it directly into the postman's eyes.

The postman screamed and dropped Barnabas. As Peter rushed to join his new friend on the pavement, he also "accidentally" sprayed the shop-keeper for good measure.

Both men stumbled around blindly in the peppery mist. As they howled in pain, the rabbits sprinted away. Peter, it seemed, was out of trouble ... for now.

Chapter Seven

Back at Nigel Basil-Jones's office, Benjamin, Flopsy, Mopsy, and Cotton-tail were all having a great time. After the billboard unveiling, the rabbits had been led back inside to the chill-out area, ready to see the office assistant lay out a large platter of delicious crudités with four separate dips. Each of the bunnies grabbed a pot of dip and after a rowdy toast, glugged the entire thing down in one. Without bothering to wipe their chops, they hastily grabbed a slice of tomato and sucked it like a lime, wrinkling their noses and wincing at the strange taste.

"That was not good," Flopsy declared.

The others agreed – those dips were indeed terrible.

Across the room, Basil-Jones had produced a heavy contract for Bea to sign. The author sat nervously at the publisher's vast desk, her pen poised, as Basil-Jones turned through the hundreds of pages, pointing out each dotted line requiring a signature ...

"... And there ... and there ... and there ... and there ... and there ... and there ... and whoops, missed one ... and there ... and there ... and there

". . . and . . . nope, that's the notary . . . and there . . . and there . . . and there . . ."

The rabbits looked over.

"Doesn't seem like the healthiest way to start a relationship," Flopsy remarked.

"And . . . a fingerprint," Basil-Jones finally concluded, flourishing an inkpad.

Bea paused. "My book is very personal to me and I don't want to compromise it," she ventured. "I would be spinning in my grave if it were ever to be adapted into some sassy hip-fest purely for commercial gain. Probably by an American."

"Sounds like someone's trying to work through something," Benjamin murmured under his breath, to no one in particular.

Basil-Jones looked Bea straight in the eyes. "I give you my word that I will be your ferocious guardian, a fortress between your art and all who wish to boorishly capitalize on it," he said sincerely.

There was again a moment's pause. The rabbits held their breath as Bea looked over to her husband.

Thomas gave a brief nod.

Bea grabbed the inkpad, rolled her finger back and forth and stamped the contract.

Nigel Basil-Jones stood up and smiled. "Of course, making it more contemporary by, say, putting the rabbits in sneakers or hoodies, would increase the readership and benefit the Land Preservation Fund . . . but to what end? You're a purist. I respect that."

"I just want to help children enjoy honest, simple pleasures," said Bea. "Nothing more."

Thomas shook his head. "Sneakers?" he snorted. "Can you even imagine?"

HONK! The sound of a car horn filtered up from the street below. Nigel Basil-Jones sauntered to the open window.

"Hi, Marvin," he yelled down. "Don't drive too fast! We need your next book!"

Bea and Thomas approached the window. They just glimpsed a man waving up from the driving seat of a sleek and shiny red convertible sports car, before he sped off down the street.

"One of our authors." Basil-Jones shrugged. "We gave him that car when his book hit number one." The publisher waved his hand at a tasteful painting of a cloud of butterflies. "Marvin wrote a book about butterflies. Gorgeous, elegant, it could hang in a museum. Sold one hundred and fifty copies. I suggested a small change . . ."

He moved to a shelf and picked up a book featuring the very same insects.

Bea blinked. The butterflies were now riding on

skateboards! Alongside the newly cool bugs there was a prominent sticker proclaiming, **#1 BESTSELLER.**

"The Queen just knighted him," Basil-Jones threw in.

Bea tried to absorb what she'd just been told, just as Flopsy looked around.

"Where's Peter?" asked Flopsy.

Bea's eyes scanned the fancy office. There was no sign of Peter Rabbit.

"I think he said something about going on a contemplative walk," replied Mopsy.

Peter was indeed strolling, deep in thought. But he certainly wasn't alone. He and Barnabas walked side by side through the back streets of Gloucester, munching on stolen muffins.

". . . You, your sisters, your cousin Benjamin. I was around a bunch," Barnabas was saying.

"I don't remember you," admitted Peter. "Sorry."

Barnabas smiled back at him. "Wouldn't expect you to. You were too young."

Peter took another bite of his muffin.

"Why'd you leave?" he said.

"Your pops and I were a team. After what

McGregor did to him – I was sure to be next."
Barnabas stopped short. They were in front of an
open door. Inside, a restaurant kitchen was in the
middle of a busy service. Through plumes of steam
curling up from the bubbling and sizzling pans,
Peter could see chefs chopping furiously, shouting
commands as they worked.

Barnabas chuckled. "He was something else,
mate. I remember one time he waltzed right into a
kitchen like that and nabbed a sweet potato. Right in
front of the cooks.'

Peter eyed the scene. Before Barnabas could say
another word, the little rabbit dashed at full pelt into
the kitchen, bounding between legs as he tore up
the aisles. A second later, he was right back at
Barnabas's side, a steaming hot sweet potato
clamped in his mouth.

"Hot! Hot! Hot!" Peter spat the scalding vegetable onto the pavement by Barnabas's feet.

The gruff old rabbit guffawed with laughter.
"You've certainly got your pops's nose for mischief."

Peter had scalded his tongue. "Tho they thay,"
he replied.

Barnabas patted Peter on the back. "It's a good
thing, son. Don't let nobody tell you different."

And it was here in this dark alley, so many miles
from his country home, that Peter Rabbit was

celebrated for doing what he had long been told off for.

"Your pops would've been proud of you," Barnabas told him. "You're a fierce, bad rabbit, just like him."

Just then a familiar voice suddenly bounced around the walls of the alley.

"Peter!"

Thomas McGregor exploded round the corner, his face a mask of worry.

"Come on!" Barnabas shouted.

Peter froze.

"Peter!" Barnabas barked again.

But now the younger rabbit was being swept up in Thomas's arms. His face, which had last seemed so indifferent, was full of concern and protective-ness. "There you are! Are you OK?"

Peter searched for Barnabas. The rabbit was shrouded in shadow farther down the alley, but he could still make out the old-timer's face.

"Can't you just be good?" Thomas implored. "For once?"

The young rabbit searched the backstreet. His eyes found Barnabas and locked on his gaze. And then Peter was carried away to rejoin the others.

"You found him. Is he OK?" asked Bea in relief.

"He's fine," reassured her husband. "But we have

to hurry to catch the last train home."

He placed Peter down with the others. "We were looking all over for you," whispered Benjamin.

Peter looked at his family, clearly holding back something as he replied. "Told you. Went for a walk."

Chapter Eight

On the train ride home, the rabbits snuggled up together on the seats, leaning into one another, mouths open, snuffling and snoring softly. Only Peter was still awake, his head turned away from the other passengers. The bunny stared out the window, lost in thought.

Across the carriage, Bea sat talking to Thomas. "I think you should spend more time with Peter," she whispered, glancing at the rabbit to check he hadn't overheard. "Feels like he might be going through something."

Thomas was out of sight and his voice, when it came, was breathless. "I mean, sure, but he is a rabbit, Bea," he panted. "He's not like our *real* child." Bea peered over the back of her seat. Thomas was lying on the carriage floor doing sit-ups!

"What are you doing?" she demanded.

Thomas kept going. "I missed my workout today," he explained.

"You miss your workout every day," said Bea.

She turned back to her book – a copy of Dickens's *A Tale of Two Cities*. It was hard to maintain the moral high ground when it was obvious that the novel had been hastily picked up at the train station shop before the trip home.

"Suddenly had the urge to read Dickens, did you?" asked Thomas.

"He's my favorite author," Bea said.

Thomas wasn't buying it. "Name one more book by Dickens," he dared her.

"Do one more sit-up," Bea shot back.

The train clattered on through the darkening countryside. Peter stayed silently staring out the window.

The next day got off to a fine and sunny start. The McGregors' hardworking cockerel, JW Rooster II, was up with the dawn ready to crow in the new morning.

"Cock-a-doodle-doo! Wake up, boys! Wake up! We have a job to do! Cock-a-doodle-doo!"

The bird yelled but his teenage sons continued to sleep.

"Aw, Dad," they whined. "We're tired . . ."

"So am I!" JW Rooster II squawked back. "But we have to make the gigantic ball of fire rise into the sky so the world gets warm and life as we know it can continue!"

The kids clucked in amazement. For real? They had no idea that they had so much responsibility! One by one, the cockerels staggered to their feet and made noisy attempts at "Cock-a-doodle-doo!"

JW Rooster II fixed his eye on the horizon. Slowly, very slowly, the sun crested over the hills behind the McGregor farm. Their work here was done.

"Now feel free to peck around doing absolutely nothing for the next twenty-four hours," he said.

Peter emerged from his burrow. The first thing he saw was Thomas in the vegetable garden tending carefully to his beloved tomatoes. Today he wasn't alone – Benjamin, Flopsy, Mopsy, and Cotton-tail were all happily helping him prune and water. It was precious time.

Family time.

Peter frowned. A family that did not include him.

As his supposed now-Dad played happy family outside with the others, Peter went to find out more about his real dad. He loped inside the cottage, where Bea was busy painting. Peter hopped over to the easel and began to look through the pictures she had already finished.

Suddenly, a painting caught his eye. It was a portrait of another rabbit. A rabbit he recognized. Peter gulped. It had to be Barnabas. A very young Barnabas.

Peter looked up at Bea, paintbrush in hand, her brow furrowed in concentration as she worked on a corner of the paper. He so wanted to ask her about Barnabas. She's the one who would have known. She was the one he could always count on.

"Peter!" she called. "Come here!"

She bent down as if to nuzzle her face against his. Instead, without warning, she grabbed his feet and slipped them into a pair of sneakers.

"That's a good boy. Now just walk over there," she said, giving him a nudge.

Peter stared at the painting that was perched on Bea's easel. All the rabbits were there, but each was wearing a pair of oversized trainers. Sportswear was obviously not Bea's strong suit – they were really badly drawn. And sometimes even moms can be preoccupied with their own stuff.

"Is this silly?" she said to herself. "This is silly. This isn't what I paint. I paint you. But Nigel must know something . . ."

Peter stumbled around. He felt taken advantage of. The shoes felt all wrong.

This. Felt. All. Wrong.

"Bea!" The voice of the man who thought Peter was nothing but trouble floated in through the open doors. "We're going for a walk."

Chapter Nine

Bea, Thomas, and the rabbits strolled through the countryside. The rabbits frolicked ahead but Benjamin waited for a moment for Flopsy, Mopsy, and Cotton-tail to run on, before falling in step with Peter.

"Ready to tell me where you went yesterday?" he said inquiringly. "You had us all worried."

"No need to worry, cousin," Peter said.

"I understand why you'd be mad," pressed Benjamin. "Labeled the bad seed on a big billboard."

Peter tried to stay calm. "I'm not mad, friend."

"You should be," said Benjamin. "You missed the crudité. Know what that is? Vegetables in the shape of *rectangles*!"

But Peter would not be distracted today – even by talk of carrot batons. "I know I have a bit of a reputation as an exaggerator, a fabricator, a falsifier . . ." He paused, expecting Benjamin to set him straight.

His cousin waited for an inordinate amount of time before the penny dropped. "I'm sorry, was I supposed to disagree?"

"A little push-back would have been nice,"

moaned Peter. "Last night I met someone who may have changed my life forever."

Benjamin's excitement levels shot skyward. "You met a girl! Yes! Yes! Tell me everything. I want to know it all! What's her name? Mary? Scarlet? Josephine?"

"Barnabas," Peter said.

"Terrific!" Benjamin replied with no judgment.

"No!" said Peter. "He's an old friend of Dad's."

"Wonderful!"

"No! Here's what happened . . ." And Peter told Benjamin all about it.

A few paces behind, Bea and Thomas were also deep in conversation.

"Think how much of this land we'll be able to preserve," said Bea, pausing to admire the spectacular view.

"All the nature our children will be able to explore," Thomas added.

Bea looked fondly at the rabbits frolicking ahead of them.

"I know." Bea smiled. "Look at them go."

"Never got to do that," Thomas said. "Not much frolicking at the group home. Which is why I also picture having some two-legged children to frolic with."

Bea put her arm tenderly around her husband.

"They'd have that whole mountain if I put trainers on the rabbits."

"Trainers!" Thomas scoffed. "Can you believe he said that?"

"I can't even paint trainers. Now, hoodies – hoodies are easier. They're really just jackets with little hats sewn on them, aren't they?"

Thomas couldn't believe Bea would even entertain the suggestion. He decided not to say anything, opting for a stern *Really?* look instead.

The rabbits hopped up the hillside. Cotton-tail dashed on ahead of her sisters, reaching the top first. She had bags of energy today – she had kept a secret stash of the fruity jelly beans from the day before. The silly rabbit popped one in her mouth, swallowed, and then with a wild-eyed look cried, "Check it out, sisters!"

Cotton-tail launched into an impressive flip and then tumbled down the hill from top to bottom.

"Should we be concerned about these magic beans she can't stop eating?" suggested Mopsy.

"I decided something," said Flopsy. "I'm changing my name so it won't rhyme with yours."

Mopsy totally agreed with this. "Fine by me," she said. "What is it?"

Flopsy puffed out her chest. "Lavatory," she announced proudly.

Mopsy was blindsided. "Lavatory?"

"Yes? You called? How can I help you? I'm fancy, from the city, very busy at all times, only run on two legs."

Mopsy did not want to burst her sister's bubble, but she had her concerns. "Where'd you get that name?" she asked.

"I saw it on the train, m'lady."

From the foot of the hill came Cotton-tail's rallying cry, "Come on! Get some speed up!"

"After you, Lavatory," Mopsy said.

"Thank you kindly," Flopsy replied, rearing up and attempting to run on two legs. Mopsy rolled her eyes and sped past her sister. She reached Cotton-tail at the bottom while Flopsy was still struggling on two feet.

"What's with her?" Cotton-tail asked.

"Changed her name to Bathroom," Mopsy explained.

Flopsy decided to give up on the two-leg running. She curled up like a furry cannonball and rolled the rest of the way down the hill, landing in a heap next to her sisters.

"I think I broke my kneecap," she moaned.

"We don't have knee caps," Cotton-tail sighed.

Flopsy jumped up. "Oh, then I'm fine."

Still at the top of the hill, Bea gestured at the tumbling bunnies.

"Go on," she urged. "Join them. Frolic."

"Really?" Thomas was not at all sure about this suggestion. "Like, stretch my arms above my head, extend my legs, lie on the ground, and tumble down the steep incline?"

"You really had a rough childhood," guessed Bea.

"I was eighteen before I found out ice cream wasn't frozen toothpaste," Thomas said, and with that he took a running jump, threw himself down on the grass, and began to roll.

It was not pretty. The air filled with screams as he picked up speed.

At the bottom, Thomas was still for a moment but then he stood up and staggered dizzily around before collapsing facedown on to the grass.

Mopsy hopped toward him. "And that's why adults shouldn't do kid stuff," she sighed.

"That was so much fun," groaned Thomas.

Chapter Ten

Peter had so much to tell Benjamin. His story about the day with Barnabas in Gloucester lasted all the way back to McGregor Manor. Benjamin wanted to hear every last, crazy detail of the adventure.

"So you sprayed pepper juice at the candy man?" Peter nodded. "I've never felt more alive, Benjamin. And this is coming from the chap who shot a bunch of balloons out of the sky and caught Bea and McGregor in midair."

"No, you didn't, Peter. You imagined that, remember?"

"Aah, yes. Right. I tend to conflate reality," Peter said, tapping his head, "and the old meat computer. But what I do know is real – I'm going back to Gloucester."

Benjamin was shocked. "Really? This Barnabas sounds a bit dodgy."

"He's not dodgy. Mischievous yeah, but so am I. And so was Dad. He gets me, Benjamin."

"I get you," Benjamin told his cousin. "That's why I'm worried you're heading down a bad path."

"Maybe that's where I belong." Peter shrugged.

Bea and Thomas decided to go out. They clambered into the Land Rover, revved the engine, and motored down the driveway. As they drew level with Peter and Benjamin, Thomas wound down his window.

"Stay out of trouble!" he yelled.

Peter turned to his cousin. "Told you he has it in for me."

"He was talking to all of us," insisted Benjamin. "It was a general expression. Like, 'good luck' or, 'keep calm and carry on.'"

But as Benjamin spoke, the Land Rover slowed, stopped briefly, and reversed back toward the rabbits. Thomas leaned out of his window and peered down at the rabbits.

"I'm talking to you, Peter," he said. "Specifically. Stay. Out. Of. Trouble."

Peter glanced at Benjamin. He said nothing, but his expression spoke volumes. "See?'

The Land Rover was just pulling away again when Peter looked at his cousin with sudden purpose. "You're in charge till I get back."

"What? No!"

Benjamin's voice was panicky.

"You'll be fine," Peter called, bounding off.

He stopped for a second and turned. "You sure that balloon thing was in my head? Because I really remember it happening. Like, vividly."

Before Benjamin could answer, Peter had leaped into the open back of the McGregors' truck.

"Wait! Peter!" Benjamin yelled as he watched the Land Rover disappear down the drive and then turn on to the road.

The bunny tried his best to gather his courage. "I'm in charge," he said. "OK. About time, if you ask me. Which I just did."

Flopsy, Mopsy, and Cotton-tail ran up.

"Where did Peter go?"

"What are we doing now?"

"What's for lunch?"

It was all already too much for Benjamin to handle.

"I don't know! I don't know! I don't know!" he replied, taking a running jump into the nearby pond and disappearing beneath the water.

The triplets strolled over and peered down into the murky gloom.

"Is he OK?" Mopsy asked.

Benjamin resurfaced but, before anyone could say anything, the harassed bunny took another deep breath and dived back down again.

A little while later, the McGregors pulled up in Windermere. Peter jumped off the truck and ran straight for the train station.

Within a couple of hours the determined bunny was back in Gloucester and walking the street where he had first encountered Barnabas. Peter turned the corner and spotted his dad's pal again. Peter didn't hesitate – he ran straight over.

Barnabas turned and saw the youngster skid to a stop beside him. "Caught the bug, did you?"

"I think I always had it," Peter said.

"There they are!"

It was the shopkeeper again, pointing the rabbits out to two other people.

Their van was parked on the street. The writing on the side read **PIPERSON'S PETS**. A man and a woman stood beside it, brandishing poles with wire loops on the end designed for only one thing: trapping runaway animals.

"Who are they?" Peter asked anxiously.

"The McGregors of the city," Barnabas replied.

The two rabbits took off, trying to avoid those poles. With a THWOOP and a WHOMP they quickly found themselves caught and then lifted inside the van. Doors clanged shut, the engine started, and the vehicle drove away.

Peter found himself being jostled and bumped through the city, stuffed alongside Barnabas in the same small crate in the back. He was terrified.

"Where are they taking us?" Peter whispered.

"Stay calm, son," Barnabas growled. "I won't let anything happen to you."

As the crate bumped up and down inside the van, Peter caught tiny glimpses of Gloucester whizzing past outside. A city that had once seemed exciting, now promised danger at every turn.

Chapter Eleven

The rabbits found themselves blinking in the sunlight as strong hands swung their crate out of the van. So they were inside a shop – Piperson's Pets.

The crate holding Peter and Barnabas was plonked on a display rack in the window. Piperson's was a small but well-stocked shop. Peter craned his neck to look around. Barnabas, meanwhile, seemed oddly calm.

A sudden scuffle and a child's high-pitched squeal made Peter freeze.

"I want that one! It's just like Peter from the book that Nana gave me," said a little girl. At the same time a small hand reached into the crate, grabbed Peter by the scruff of the neck, and pulled him out.

Peter glanced back down at Barnabas, still trapped in the crate. The pair stared at each other and, as the girl turned away with her new pet, Barnabas reached out a paw and grabbed Peter's leg.

"Aw," gasped the girl, "they want to go together. Can I get this one, too, Mum? Please? They look like father and son."

The girl's mother looked at the pair. "More like

'before and *after*,'" she said begrudgingly. "All right then, go on."

Peter and Barnabas were driven to their new home, to assume their roles as pets to Amelia, the little girl.

Amelia insisted on carrying the crate in all by herself. The bunnies clung to the bars like a shipwreck in a storm, as the cage lurched back and forth. Peter caught sight of himself on the cover of Bea's book as they swung past a bookshelf before, WHAM! Amelia slammed the crate down on the floor.

Amelia's brother, Liam, ran in. Together the children took the rabbits out of the cage.

"I'm naming mine Monkey Boo-Boo," Amelia cried, tossing a terrified Peter into the air.

"Mine's called Mrs. Yogurt-Face," Liam yelled, throwing Barnabas skyward, too. The rabbits peered at each other as they passed in midair. Peter's face screamed, *What do we do!*

For the next hour, Amelia and Liam had a wonderful time playing with their new pets. Thomas and Barnabas, however, did not have a great time. They were prodded, pulled, tweaked, nuzzled, and squeezed.

The children even raided their toy box. The rabbits found themselves sporting sunglasses and hats, then stuffed into toy cars and raced at breakneck speed down a steep flight of stairs.

If all that wasn't enough, the rabbits were then pitted against each other in a manic dance-off. Peter was shocked to see Barnabas play along. More than play along – the older rabbit had some serious moves!

Barnabas twirled, taking off his top hat with a flourish to cover his mouth.

"Just give 'em what they want, son," he whispered quietly.

Then offering his paw, which Peter took, he pulled him into the dance, too. Soon the pair of them were spinning and swishing, jumping and jiving in a most entertaining show.

Amelia and Liam loved it. "Yay!"

"Mum, can the bunnies sleep in my room?" Amelia asked sweetly at the end.

"Not until they get their shots," came the short and not-so-sweet reply.

Shots? Peter made wide-eyed, panicked faces at Barnabas.

There was no time to discuss it, though, as, without warning, the children shoved the rabbits back into the cage and double-locked it – just in case.

They turned out the lights, shut the door of the room, and left, leaving the rabbits in pitch-darkness. A tiny chink of light under the door allowed Peter to make out Barnabas lying in the cage. Peter gulped and caught his breath.

"You all right, son?"

"This is what it's like to be a pet?"

Peter could hardly believe he was saying these words out loud.

"It ain't pretty."

"What do we do now?" Peter asked.

"We go to work," said Barnabas.

Peter looked up. The door to the cage was open, and his buddy was standing on the outside.

Barnabas winked, then headed out of the room. Peter was in disbelief but followed his friend.

Chapter Twelve

Back in Windermere, Thomas McGregor and Bea were working at the toyshop. Thomas was busy repairing the window Peter had broken during the encounter with his fans.

"And he's handy, too," boomed a voice. "Is there nothing this man can't do?"

It was Nigel Basil-Jones. The publisher swept farther into the store, clapped Thomas on the back, and began throwing punches at him.

Thomas was startled. He had forgotten about Basil-Jones's boxing credentials and did not have time to brace before the blows.

"Ah, it's just a quick fix," he winced, trying to cover the fact that those punches had really hurt.

"Thomas," called Bea as she wandered into the shop, "can I call the glass man? You've been at it for six hours!"

"Mr. Basil-Jones," she exclaimed. "What a nice surprise!"

Cotton-tail's head snapped up with a fiendish look on her face. She gasped.

"Beans. Beans. The bean man's back."

The bunny rushed over to Basil-Jones and began

pawing aggressively at his pockets.

The publisher was completely unperturbed by the effect his gift basket sweeties had wreaked on the rabbit.

"Hello to you, too, little cutie," he said gently, before turning to Bea and asking whether it was a good time.

"It's the best of times, it's the worst of times . . . ," Bea quoted, in her most literary voice.

There was confused silence.

"Dickens."

Nigel Basil-Jones set his briefcase down and removed a hardcover book. "I couldn't wait to show you this."

Bea and Thomas stared at the copy of *Peter Rabbit*. This new Basil-Jones Publishing version of Bea's story was absolutely beautiful. Her illustration of the blue-jacketed rabbit shone from the glossy cover. The design was glorious. The font classy. A triumph.

"Wow!" breathed Bea.

"It's incredible," gasped Thomas.

"We've had a tremendous response," Basil-Jones said. "Interest in your book is already through the roof."

Bea flipped to the author photo gazing out of the dust jacket. There she was, or at least there was a very glossy, staged version of Bea staring out from the jacket flap. She had perfect makeup, an over-the-top outfit, and beautifully blow-dried hair that was being fashionably whipped by the wind.

"When did you take this?" Thomas asked.

"I don't even remember – I think it was just lying around," Bea mumbled.

In truth, the shoot to produce this picture had taken place in their bedroom while Thomas slept, had lasted several hours, and involved racks of clothes, banks of lights, blowing fans, and the photographic skills of a sleepy Peter Rabbit, who'd been woken up and roped in to take the shots.

But Bea wasn't going to admit how hard she had worked on it. "I have something for you, too," she said, deftly changing the subject. She popped behind the counter and returned with a painting. She handed it to Nigel.

The painting was pure Bea. It showed an ordinary garden scene featuring her beloved bunnies. Only one change had been made – the rabbits were all wearing hoodies.

"You can barely tell the difference, right?" She smiled hopefully. "Is it a hat? Is it a hood?"

Thomas was incredulous. "You actually did it?"

Nigel Basil-Jones clapped his hands together in delight. "It's brilliant. Artistic, authentic, uncompromising and . . . hmm . . . Where is that?"

"Our garden," Bea replied.

"A bit limited in scope, no?"

"But that's where they live."

"I just thought," crooned Basil-Jones in honeyed tones, "since you gave them hoodies you might want to age it up. Make it fun, exotic – maybe put them on a beach? Give them surfboards, those little baby guitars . . ."

"Ukuleles?" Bea asked.

"Yes! What a great idea! See? You take my dopey suggestions and make them so much better. Genius."

Thomas felt an urgent need to inject some sanity into the conversation.

"They don't play ukuleles, don't go to the beach. They're rabbits."

Basil-Jones was having none of this pesky *reality* nonsense. "Why can't there be rabbits on a beach?" he demanded. "Or a boat? Or a rocket ship? Readers want to be transported."

He pointed to the **30% DONATED TO LAND PRESERVATION** sign above the till. "It will be great for your fund," he added silkily. Basil-Jones brought a bulging bag of colorful jelly beans out of his pocket. "Oh, I brought you more of these. You ate a tremendous amount last time."

Cotton-tail made a lunge for the beans, but Benjamin, Flopsy, and Mopsy held her back.

"Keep up the good work, you two," Basil-Jones said, and he walked out, slamming the door.

CRASH! The glass pane in the window shattered into a million pieces.

In a house somewhere in Gloucester, Peter Rabbit was following his friend. He inched warily into the kitchen and found Barnabas sizing up an enormous refrigerator.

"No handles," the rabbit said. "Terrific. We got adopted by a family of artsy-fartsies."

Barnabas ran his paw down the door, placing his ear against the cool metal. With the skill of a safe cracker, he located the sweet spot, breathed on it, and then marked an *X* in the condensation. Peter watched in awe. Without a word Barnabas took a few steps back from the fridge and then dashed forward and leaped at the cross, hitting it with both feet at the same time.

Bullseye! As if by magic, the door swung open.

Barnabas climbed in and began ransacking the shelves.

"Putting tomatoes in the fridge?" he exclaimed,

brandishing an unripened one. "And they call *us* animals?"

Peter, meanwhile, started piecing things together. "You wanted to get taken to that pet shop . . . You wanted them to adopt you so you could rob them . . ."

Barnabas was unapologetic. "Lot less dangerous than sneaking into McGregor's garden, mate. And *this* was our land once, too."

And with that, the gruff old rabbit began tossing food out to Peter. The youngster skillfully caught an apple and took a bite. He threw it back to Barnabas, who also chomped down on it. Their game of catch and chew continued until the apple was just a core, which was discarded.

When he'd finished with the fridge, Barnabas moved into the pantry. He tossed a can to Peter, who winced at the picture of a dog on it. But Barnabas indicated to him to turn it around – it was just dog food. Peter sighed in relief as Barnabas moved on to the children's lunch boxes that stood prepared on the side.

He expertly popped each box open to reveal chocolate bars, cheese, and chips. The old-timer pushed those aside in favor of slices of juicy apple and pre-cut crunchy carrot.

Barnabas had evidently done this many times

before. "Kids don't eat this stuff," he muttered sagely. "It's just there to make their parents feel good about themselves."

When they'd both had their fill, Barnabas moved toward the giant dishwasher. "Wanna take a steam?" he asked.

Peter watched, confused, as Barnabas opened the appliance up then hit a button with his paw. He lay down on the bottom rack of the dishwasher, gesturing for Peter to join him.

Steam began to curl in cleansing swirls around the rabbits, caressing their fur with warm air. Peter felt his whole body relax.

". . . and what is bad, really?" he said sleepily. "And what is good? And who's to say someone's *good* can't be someone's *bad*?"

"I've been wrestling with that my whole life, partner," Barnabas replied.

He looked over to Peter. The little rabbit had fallen asleep in their makeshift steamroom. "Yeah," Barnabas smiled, "you gotta work up to this setting."

The old rabbit kicked the door of the dishwasher open and while Peter slumbered on, jumped out. He leaped up to the window, performed an adept reverse handstand, then shoved it open with his feet. Barnabas leaned out, then rasped, "Whiskers!"

Chapter Thirteen

A small brown rat rubbed his paws greedily then stepped out from the shadows, beady eyes darting left and right up the street. Samuel Whiskers wore a button waistcoat and a shabby tweed jacket, his little pink tail trailing behind. Although he looked like somebody's bumbling uncle, this was not a gentleman to be trusted. He had once rolled a kitten up in pastry and tried to eat him for supper.

And that kitten was Tom Kitten. The unfortunate cat had only lived to tell the tale because of his sister, Mittens. Mittens had rescued Tom from his pastry-dough prison and then together the pair had beat the living cheese out of Samuel Whiskers. The bashing he received on that fateful day had been a most unpleasant experience, but it had earned the old rat's respect. Now the three thieves were bonded for life.

Tom Kitten and Mittens duly appeared on the pavement beside Samuel.

Everyone knew the drill. First the kittens rolled out a children's stroller, parking it just below the window. Next Barnabas began hurling food down for the pair to catch and stow.

Up above, Peter had roused from his steam bath. He quickly saw what was going on and did his best to help out. Tasty loot in all shapes and sizes rained out of the window.

"My pickup crew," the old rabbit explained, gesturing to the rogues below. "Followed us from the pet shop. Job's worth nothing without the get-away."

Peter blinked. "They just walk down the street pushing a stroller full of food?"

Barnabas flashed him a grin. The country boy still had a lot to learn about the way things worked in the city!

A moment later, a short man wearing a trench coat and hat awkwardly made his way down the street, pushing a buggy in front of him. He managed to pick a path along the pavement, swerving to avoid pedestrians coming the other way. Once the fellow got the hang of things, he even managed to tip his hat politely at passersby.

"I can't believe this actually works!" squeaked a voice from inside the coat.

"People are lost in their own worlds," replied another voice. "Real shame what's become of society."

"You did good, son," added a third. "Felt like old times with your pops."

It appeared that the man was talking to himself. In different voices. Except of course, he wasn't . . .

Inside the coat and hat, two rabbits, two kittens and a plump rat were balanced precariously on one another's shoulders. Together they formed a whole person. It was ingenious. Audacious. And rather uncomfortable.

"Why am I always the leg?" demanded Tom Kitten, from somewhere near the bottom.

Peter could barely believe what they were trying to get away with. But as he wobbled along the street, he felt part of something for the very first time in a while. He belonged.

"Oi! That's my coat!"

An angry shout shattered Peter's newfound calm. A furious, real-life man was running to catch up with them. Amelia's father!

"Those woodland animals are standing atop each other and impersonating a human!" he bellowed.

Barnabas gave a new command. "Scramble."

The thieves made a desperate dash for it. Their pretend man and the buggy lolloped along the street in great gaping strides, his top half lurching from side to side. It was a floppy sight. As they turned into a lane that curved toward a tailor's shop, the animals jumped out one by one, leaving only the kittens as the legs. Barnabas and Whiskers heaved open a hatch leading down to a cellar, while Peter dumped the stroller.

Amelia's father skidded around the corner, running blindly toward the now headless and body-less man. He lurched forward and yanked the coat away, just as the kittens slithered down the hatch and out of sight.

The shop door opened. An old man appeared, wearing a tape measure around his neck. Amelia's father, sweaty and confused, stared down at the tailor.

"Need that altered, sir?" he asked helpfully.

Bea, of course, hadn't the faintest idea what perilous, real-life exploits her best bunny was embroiled in. She was too busy dreaming up make-believe adventures for him instead. She had been holed up in her art studio for hours, painting watercolor after watercolor of Peter and his family.

It was safe to say that Bea had decided to take a new direction with her work. Instead of scenes in the vegetable patch, her pictures showed bunnies playing ukuleles on the beach, skiing down mountains, and in one particularly ambitious piece, white-water rafting.

Benjamin and the triplets eyed the paintings, utterly mystified.

"I'm no art critic," said Benjamin, "but these seem banana-pants crazy."

Flopsy frowned at Mopsy. "Why is she painting us the same height?"

"Because we are the same height, Flopsy."

Flopsy huffed. "You may be the same height as *Flopsy*, whoever *she* is," she remarked airily, "but I'm *Lavatory*, and I'm quite a bit taller than you."

And just to prove the point, Flopsy got up on her tippy-toes and teetered away.

"Lavatory?" muttered Benjamin. "Does she know what that means?"

Mopsy shook her head. "No. And that's what makes us different – I know and she doesn't."

Cotton-tail stayed out of the argument. Instead, Benjamin and Mopsy found her licking madly at the dry water bowl.

"Why is there no water?" she rasped. "Why? Why!"

"Because you drank it all," Benjamin reminded her. "Which is what happens when you eat too much sugar."

"I didn't eat any sugar. Just hundreds and

hundreds of those sweet, syrupy, sweet beans."

"You know what happens next, right?" sighed Benjamin.

Cotton-tail didn't answer. She had already fallen asleep standing up.

"That."

Just then, Thomas McGregor arrived. He was cradling an egg carton in front of him, filled with perfect, ripe tomatoes.

"I think my tomatoes are ready! I want honest opinions from everyone," he declared, before noticing Cotton-tail's little slumped figure. "She OK?"

Flopsy gave Cotton-tail a nudge. She woke up with a start.

But something even more shocking had grabbed Thomas's attention. He stared, aghast, at Bea's paintings.

"You're really putting them on the beach?" he asked, moving along the line of watercolors. "Are they white-water rafting? Is that a cruise ship?"

Bea was defensive. "I'm just expanding our world," she replied.

"But that's not our world," said Thomas.

"No," countered Bea, "it's bigger than our world. And look how happy the rabbits are."

Thomas looked down at the floor, his eyes

82

moving from bunny to bunny. But Bea was pointing at her paintings.

"But . . . those are paintings," he said quietly.

"Exactly," said Bea. "Nigel is really pushing me to explore my imagination. Everyone's seen rabbits. But have they seen them on a rocket ship in space?"

"No, but do you think there might be a reason they've never seen them on a rocket ship in space?" Thomas ventured.

"Maybe it's because I haven't painted it yet," she mused. "Nigel wants me to – "

"I know what Nigel wants, but is this what you want?"

Bea had an epiphany!

"Mason jars."

"What?" spluttered Thomas.

But Bea was already running out of the cottage. "For their space helmets!" she called happily over her shoulder.

Thomas groaned. Bea was gone and he hadn't even got to show off his tomatoes. He went to fetch some water for the rabbits.

"Nigel," he grumbled, filling up their bowl. "Just because he is successful, intelligent, charismatic, eyes you could lose an afternoon in . . . He needs to hear from me. Stay out of trouble," he warned the rabbits. "Although I guess I don't have to say that because Peter's not here." Thomas looked around the cottage. "Where is he?"

There was a pregnant pause.

"And once again I find myself talking to rabbits and awaiting a response that . . ."

Benjamin and the triplets stared up at Mr McGregor, their noses twitching expectantly.

"Nope," he muttered, following after Bea. "Not forthcoming."

But as soon as Thomas had gone, Flopsy wanted answers.

"Where is Peter?" she asked.

"Benjamin saw him last," Cotton-tail replied.

Flopsy, Mopsy, and Cotton-tail turned to their cousin expectantly.

"As the interim leader of this family," Benjamin began, pulling himself up to his full height, "there are certain things I must protect you from. Sometimes not knowing is the wisest form of . . ."

The girls glared at him.

"*Gloucester*. He's in *Gloucester*."

"Why?" Mopsy demanded.

"Again," attempted Benjamin, "the burden of responsibility precludes me from sharing sensitive information that might cause you to . . . He met a thief who was *a friend of your dad's*."

Flopsy's ears pricked up. "We have to go and get him."

"No!" gasped Benjamin. "And with this I put my foot down once and for – " But then, out of the corner of his eye, he spotted Thomas marching toward his Land Rover. Who was he kidding? *"We better hurry, though, because Mr McGregor is heading for Gloucester, I see him pulling out right now."*

The rabbits tore out of the cottage. It was time for Peter to come home.

Chapter Fourteen

Peter was holed up underneath a tailor's shop. The table in front of him was positively groaning with loot, the spoils of the pet shop job.

"Baboom," said Tom Kitten, two-hand-pointing at Peter.

Not wanting to be impolite, Peter two-hand-pointed back.

Tom Kitten was appalled. "What are you doing?"

"No, you pointed at me, so I pointed back," said Peter, "because I thought it was like a cool, pointy *Go team!* gesture."

Samuel's eyes flicked toward the table. "He was pointing at the tuna, kid," he muttered. "He's a cat."

Oh. Peter located the can of fish and tossed it over to Tom. He then passed it wearily to Mittens, who bit the lid open with her fangs.

Samuel held out his paws. "And for me?"

Peter scanned the bounty, suddenly feeling nervous. He didn't want to get this wrong! At last he spotted a slab of cheese. He passed it across to Whiskers.

"That's a good bunny," he said, giving him an approving nod.

Mittens pointed at Peter. "It's fun being bad, innit?"

But when the newcomer didn't respond, her smirk turned into a snarl. "What, you don't point back?"

"Oh no," cried Peter, leaping up from his seat. "I thought that, because last time he pointed and I misconstrued – "

Samuel motioned for him to relax. "She's kidding. Relax. Eat a grape."

"Tuck in, son," agreed Barnabas. "You earned it. You're one of us now."

As Peter chowed down with his new friends, he was in heaven.

"And I think with this haul, we earned a night out," added Mittens. "Eh, boss?"

As soon as it got dark, the gang was on the move again across the city to the waterfront. They headed toward two squirrels loitering in front of an abandoned lighthouse boat. One by one, the animals crept along the gangplank and made their way inside.

Down below deck, the boat was like another world. All of the coolest creatures of Gloucester seemed to have gathered here – mice, cats, rabbits, even pigs were all hanging out and having fun. There was dancing, feasting, and gambling. It was the wildest thing Peter had ever seen!

As they walked through the party, Peter noticed how the animals became quiet, clearing the way for the group to go by. Barnabas and his crew were respected here. Eyes watched and Peter flushed with pride as the rabbit introduced him to everyone.

The chatter resumed and the crew gathered around the ninepin alley. Barnabas took aim, then deftly bowled a crab apple toward a neat set of pinecones. Strike! A cheer went up. Whiskers sprang forward to claim his winnings – a crunchy pile of almonds – leaving Peter to watch on with Tom and Mittens.

"You really rolled him up in dough?" he asked, still not quite able to believe it.

Samuel gave a brisk nod. "Food was scarce in them days."

"I still have nightmares," sighed Tom. "Bibibity."

"You know what that's like, right, rabbit?" chipped in Mittens.

Barnabas looked earnestly at Peter. "After

your pops, I joined a support group for pastry-dough survivors."

"There is such a thing?"

Barnabas gestured toward a porthole where a group of animals were sitting in a circle of tiny folding chairs. Each was clutching a coffee-stained paper cup and listening intently to a pig standing in the center of the group.

"My name's Little Pig Robinson," he began with some difficulty. "I was put in puff pastry."

"Hi, Little Pig," the others chorused.

Wow. Peter had an uneasy feeling that he was intruding. He turned back and focused on Barnabas instead.

"Lots to show you, son." The old-timer smiled. "Whole world out there."

Barnabas picked up another crab apple and placed it firmly into Peter's paw.

The pinecones were set up and waiting. Peter hopped toward the nine-pin alley and took aim.

Strike!

Peter's heart leaped in his chest as the crowd went nuts.

Not so far away, Thomas McGregor had made it into

town. As the Land Rover turned toward Basil-Jones's office, the bunnies spotted the giant billboard advertising Bea's book.

"Never gets old," Flopsy admitted.

Benjamin peered down the street. This was their cue to leave Thomas and strike out in search of Peter.

"Let's go," he whispered.

Flopsy, Mopsy, and Cotton-tail jumped out of the truck. As they leaped toward the curb, Thomas noticed a flash of white in his rearview mirror. *That wasn't a rabbit?* he pondered. *Surely not?* He quickly dismissed the ridiculous notion and concentrated on the road.

Once Thomas was out of sight, the bunnies had some decisions to make.

"How are we going to find Peter?" wondered Mopsy.

"Well ...," replied Benjamin, trying to take charge. "We could take that street. Or that street. Then there's that street. But he might have taken an alley. There's that alley!"

The triplets had stopped listening after option one. Instead they hopped toward a small mouse, busking with his quartet under a street lamp, leaving Benjamin pondering the various options.

"Johnny!" cried Cotton-tail.

Johnny Town-mouse's crooning trailed away to nothing.

"The famous bunnies!" he frowned. "I've only been busting my tail since I was a pup. Music school, taking any gig I can get, disappointing my parents – but you just bunk up next to a lady with a paint-brush and you've made it!"

"It's going to happen for you, too, one day, Johnny, I know it," said Mopsy.

"*Don't*," said Johnny. "Just don't."

Cotton-tail hopped over. "Have you seen Peter?"

"He's down by the docks. But watch yourself, it's a bit of a rough scene," warned the little mouse, bracing himself and getting back to his perfor-mance. "Now if you'll excuse me, I have to get back to living the dream."

The triplets rushed away. They sprang past Benjamin, who was busy still talking himself through all the options.

"Now those power lines seem like a thorough-fare," he continued. "There's that one and . . ."

Benjamin looked up, finally spotting the girls disappearing into the distance.

". . . or we could go that way," he agreed, decid-ing that that might be best.

Thomas climbed out of his truck and slammed the door. He was a man on a mission. He spotted his quarry soon enough – there was Nigel Basil-Jones, as bold as brass, leaving the office in his gym clothes.

"Thomas, hi!" he beamed, infuriatingly polite as always. "What a lovely surprise."

"I know what you're up to," Mr. McGregor declared. "And don't look at me with those eyes of yours."

Nigel put his hands up. "You got me. Sneaking off to the gym for a few rounds. You box," he said at last. "Come with me."

With that, Nigel took off, leaving Thomas to follow him.

"No, I need to speak to you right now," he tried to insist. "Besides, I don't have my gear."

Basil-Jones was a very difficult person to say no to. "Not to worry," he piped up cheerfully. "We'll fix you up."

Within a few minutes Thomas was fixed up good and proper. He emerged from the locker room in short-shorts, a tank top, and an ocean of white skin. Men and women openly stared. Everybody else in the gym was toned, decked out in lycra, and mildly amused.

"Excuse me," said Thomas, dying on the inside

as he pushed his way through the sweaty bodies. "Sorry. My fault. You're very strong. Wow. Pardon me. Non-combatant here. Passing through. Whoop, got some sweat in my mouth, not mine, all good. Sorry, sorry ..."

He finally reached Nigel and climbed into the ring.

"No better place to chin-waggle than between the ropes," called the publisher, inviting him to spar. Thomas climbed in and the men began to circle each other.

"It's about Bea," said Thomas. "I'd like you to stop putting ideas in her head."

"They're good ideas," countered Nigel, bobbing left and right. "Based on years of success."

Thomas ducked, then threw a punch of his own. "They're not her ideas," he pressed. "She's losing her way."

Nigel didn't break a sweat. "Losing your way is when no one buys your book because it is too niche."

The jabs were getting harder now.

"It's *nitch*," barked Thomas, "and losing your way is when you want children because you never had a childhood yourself but your wife is too busy painting pictures of rabbits going into space!"

Nigel dropped his gloves for a moment, his interest truly piqued. "Space? Really?"

Without thinking, Thomas wound back and then clocked the publisher in the face. He gasped in surprise as Basil-Jones staggered toward the ropes.

"Oh, Nigel!" he winced. "I'm sorry."

Basil-Jones shook it off.

"No, no, I'm sorry, Thomas," he said sincerely. "Here I am focused on children's books while you're actually focused on children."

Thomas suddenly felt deflated. "I'm sorry. I shouldn't put this all on you. And are you sure you're OK? I got you pretty good."

"Nope, I've been out of line," replied Nigel. "The last thing I want to do is come between you and Bea. And from what I've seen with you and the rabbits, you'll make a great father."

Ding! Ding! Suddenly the bell was ringing.

"Good round, mate," said Thomas, glad to have straightened things out. "Sorry again about the old left cross, it's kind of what I was known for back in the day."

But as he went in for a hug, Basil-Jones was raising his gloves one more time.

"That was the start bell," he pointed out helpfully.

Chapter Fifteen

Back inside the abandoned lighthouse boat, the party was now in full swing. A rather rowdy crowd of animals were enjoying a bare-knuckled boxing match and Peter was among the spectators. He winced as a tough-looking alley cat rained down punches on what appeared to be a poor defenseless squirrel.

"Thought you said he was going to win," Peter said, turning to Barnabas.

"Wait for it," the older rabbit replied.

In a flash, the squirrel was back on her feet. A quick set of jabs sent the cocky alley cat flying through the air. She landed with a thud. The crowd went wild. Peter joined in the celebrations, unaware that more partygoers had arrived just in time to see the end of the match.

Johnny Town-mouse's information had led Flopsy, Mopsy, Cotton-tail, and Benjamin to the docks, where one rabbit was itching to have a go in the ring herself.

"I got next! I got next!" Cotton-tail yelled.

Mopsy looked at her sister and sighed. "Oh no. She's back on the beans."

But Flopsy wasn't about to be distracted from their mission. Determinedly, she sauntered up to a squirrel.

"Excuse me," she said. "Have you seen a young rabbit named Peter?"

The squirrel turned and looked Flopsy up and down. "All I see is a pretty rabbit named ..."

"Lavatory," Flopsy replied breathlessly. She was clearly smitten, and clearly distracted.

"What an elegant name." The squirrel was just reaching to kiss her hand when Mopsy interrupted.

"So *have* you seen him or *haven't* you, squirrel?" she snapped impatiently.

Meanwhile, Benjamin had spotted an overturned wooden dinghy and was fancying himself a sailor in another life.

Peter and Benjamin were still in the cheering crowd.

"This is the best night of my life," Peter ventured.

"First of many," Barnabas agreed.

"No more getting in trouble for everything." Peter nodded. "Told who I am is wrong ..."

"This is who you are, son," said Barnabas confidently. "Where you belong."

At that moment, Little Pig Robinson introduced the next challenger.

"From the hill country ... Cotton-tail!"

For a moment, Peter couldn't believe his ears. He turned to see Cotton-tail entering the fray.

"That's my sister!" Peter exclaimed.

Barnabas looked at the new opponent and frowned. "Not for long," he replied. "That squirrel's going to crack her like a nut."

Without pause, the pair lunged through the crowd and bounded into the ring. To boos and jeers, they swept up Cotton-tail from the advancing squirrel champion and dragged her outside. Benjamin and the others, having heard the ruckus, followed behind.

Once everyone was safe, Peter spoke to his family incredulously.

"What are you doing here?" he asked.

Benjamin looked at him in a matter-a-fact sort of way.

"Looking for you."

Back at the McGregor Manor, things weren't right at all. JW Rooster II was once more attempting to cajole his brood into performing their daily task. But his teenage children remained steadfastly asleep. Resigned, the rooster hopped onto the fence and began his morning ritual ... alone.

"Cock-a-aagghghgh . . . ," he coughed and spluttered. Clearing his throat, he tried again. "Cock-a-agghghghggh . . ."

Nope, it was no good. The rooster grasped his throat with his wing as a look of panic streaked across his beak. He tried to nudge his children awake but the only sound he could muster was a whisper.

"I've lost my voice! Get up! Get up!" he croaked.

His children grumbled in their sleep and turned over. It was at that moment, that a ray of sunshine broke over the horizon and bathed JW Rooster II in a warm, yellow light. He froze as he looked up at the rising sun . . .

"What?" he whispered in a strained voice. "No . . . how is this possible? It got up all by itself! It was all a sham! A lie to keep me from questioning everything. My life means nothing. I have no purpose."

And with that, he hopped down from the fence.

But JW Rooster III took his place.

"Cock-a-doodle-doo! Cock-a-doodle-doo!" he bellowed. But only the sound of the sprinklers filled the fresh country air. He looked around for a long time. "Where is everybody?" he wondered.

Someone who wasn't alone was Peter. In the city, Barnabas regaled the rabbits with tales of their father's antics. The family listened in awe.

"... and then your pops looked McGregor dead in the eye and says, 'You touch my family, I'll put you in a pie.'"

"He talked in front of a human?" Flopsy asked.

"Yeah, but it backfired on him," Barnabas replied. "It gave McGregor the idea to ... well, you know, put him in a pie. That's why we don't talk in front of humans."

"Dad was so cool," sighed Cotton-tail.

"One of the greats," Barnabas agreed, looking around at his captive audience. "I see a lot of him in you all."

"And now I've stepped in his shoes. If he wore shoes. Which he didn't." Peter looked at Barnabas. "Right? No shoes?"

"Nah. Never shoes," the older rabbit agreed.

"You should see some of the stuff we've stolen," Peter announced dramatically. "I had an *almond* yesterday."

"Whoa! No way! What did it taste like?" his sisters chorused.

"It had a warm mouthfeel, with a dry, oaty aftertaste and just the subtlest grace note of horse manure," Peter mused.

"That wasn't an almond, son," Barnabas admitted.

Peter nodded. "Ah, that explains the grace note."

His sisters seemed most impressed as Barnabas went on to sing their brother's pilfering praises.

"Your brother's a natural," Barnabas continued. "Pulled some of my biggest hauls thanks to him."

Cotton-tail, not one to miss out on an adventure, was keen to get in on the action.

"I want to pull a haul. Can I pull a haul? What's a haul?" she asked. But Benjamin had decided enough was enough by this point.

"No, no," he pressed. "No hauls. Not a good idea."

Peter, ever the protective brother, agreed. "Benjamin's right. It's much too dangerous for you."

"You did say you used to raid McGregor's garden together ... and there is something we've been wanting to do for a long time, we just haven't had a big enough crew," Barnabas began tentatively.

"You're looking at your crew! We're your crew!" Cotton-tail pressed.

"Please?" said Flopsy. "Tell us."

Barnabas looked at the rabbits, considering each one individually and replied, "Not out here."

Chapter Sixteen

While the rabbits roamed the streets of Gloucester, Bea was giving a reading of *Peter Rabbit* to a crowd of fans in a nearby bookshop.

"So Peter and the others fixed up the cottage and they all lived happily ever after," she finished, closing the book and putting it on her lap.

Rapturous applause broke out as Bea basked in her moment in the spotlight.

"Thank you," she said, smiling. "Your admiration really should be for the rabbits. I'm just their biographer."

"Where are the rabbits?" someone called out from the crowd.

"Oh, they're back in their burrow, snug as a bug in a rug," she assured everyone.

Little did Bea know that at that moment the rabbits were certainly not in their cozy burrow – they were enjoying a warehouse party.

But Bea continued to delight her readers.

"Your book is amazing," said one woman.

"Just wait till the next one," Bea replied. She put her hands to her head and mimed it exploding with ideas. The woman wasn't too sure what this gesture meant and left looking rather confused.

At that moment, Nigel stepped forward from the sidelines.

"You're a natural!" he exclaimed. "Come on, I have something to show you." He led Bea outside to reveal a shiny convertible parked at the side of the road.

Bea's convertible zoomed through Gloucester's busy streets with Nigel in the passenger seat.

"You're giving this to me?" she asked from behind the wheel.

"You deserve it," said Nigel, nodding. "The changes you're making to the new book are genius. Space? Brilliant!"

Bea turned to Nigel excitedly. "Ooh, I had an idea," said Bea. "The rabbits sneak into a moon garden and Flopsy, Mopsy, and Cotton-tail eat too many lettuces and get upset tummies."

Nigel shifted in his seat uncomfortably but encouraged her to continue with a small smile.

"So Peter and Benjamin go on a mission to find a cure, which turns out to be ... chamomile tea!"

Nigel plastered a smile on his face.

"I love it!" he said. "But they're in space, why not take advantage of that? Have you seen Marvin's latest?"

He didn't pause for breath as he reached behind to find something in the back seat of the car. It was a copy of *Butterflies vs. Zombies: The Butterflocalypse*.

"Wow. Is it good?" asked Bea.

Nigel replied, "Critics don't love it. But it just hit number one in twenty-three countries. Including Germany. And they hate butterflies. Find them too whimsical. I want you to meet the whole company. All the department heads – branding, merchandising, film. We don't just see this as a book anymore, we think it's a phenomenon."

"I can't thank you enough," she breathed. "You and Thomas are the only two people who ever really, truly believed in me."

"Thomas sure has a funny way of showing it," Nigel snorted.

"What?"

"He came to see me, didn't he tell you?" Nigel replied. "He was very upset. He actually took a swing at me."

Bea's mouth dropped open with shock.

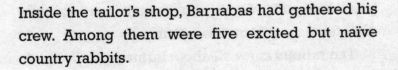

Inside the tailor's shop, Barnabas had gathered his crew. Among them were five excited but naïve country rabbits.

"It's a job," Barnabas told them. "Here in the city."

"A big job," Mittens agreed.

"The biggest," Samuel Whiskers affirmed.

"The kind of job that, if we pull it off," said Barnabas, "you'll never have to worry about feeding yourself again."

"*Popadapop*," chimed in Tom Kitten.

The rabbits were almost hopping up and down with excitement.

"Yes!" squealed Flopsy.

Mopsy shouted, "We're in!" at the same time.

Cotton-tail was just as eager as her sisters.

"Sweet," she replied.

But Barnabas felt it only fair to explain that the mission wouldn't be an easy one.

"I have to warn you, though," he pressed, "it comes with a fair bit of risk."

"Don't care!" chorused the triplets. "We're in!"

Beside the sisters, Benjamin was feeling a little less sure . . .

"Would it be all right if I heard the idea prior to summarily signing off?" he asked.

"Your uncle always said you were the smart one," Barnabas replied. "There's a place, right here in the city, where all the farmers in the valley gather at the same time . . . ," Barnabas continued.

The rabbits knew all about farmers.

"They bring their harvests with them," said Barnabas. The rabbits began to picture piles of the most luscious fruits and vegetables you'd ever seen. "And only the ripest radishes, the sweetest strawberries . . . the cream of the crop. Literally."

"Must be really hard to break in," suggested Peter, imagining a farmer pouring out jugs of cream.

Barnabas shook his head. "Not a gate or door in sight. They wave you in with a smile."

"Won't they hear us?" asked Benjamin, still feeling uncertain about the plan.

"Nah," said Barnabas confidently. "We can make all the ruckus we want because there's a band."

"What if we want to buy a handmade gift for an office gift-exchange?" Flopsy asked.

Barnabas was ready with an answer as quick as a flash. "They sell rosemary-scented candles and lavender bath bombs."

He smiled as Flopsy swooned at the very thought.

"What is this magical place?" breathed Mopsy.

"They call it . . . the farmers' market!" Barnabas declared. "But the produce ain't what we're after. Any chump with a stump can steal that."

He carried on. "What we want is far more valuable. And that's what makes this darn near impossible."

He went on to explain that at the heart of the

market stood a stall overflowing with bins of every kind of dried fruit imaginable. High above a sign read: **NAKAMOTO FAMILY FARM — DRIED FRUITS**

"We want the dried fruit," Barnabas stated.

After a confused pause, the country rabbits had some questions.

"Dried fruit?" asked Flopsy.

Cotton-tail looked equally as unimpressed. "Sounds gross."

"Why would we want that?" Mopsy exclaimed.

At this point, Whiskers took a piece of dried pineapple and held it up to the light. It glinted like a diamond in the sunlight.

"Lasts forever," he said. "And it's only an eighth of the size of a piece of fresh fruit."

"But with the same nutritional value," piped in Tom Kitten.

"Plus, it's easy to transport and totally untraceable," Mittens said, nodding.

"Ska-bosh," added Tom Kitten.

Barnabas tossed some dried fruit to the rabbits and they each took a bite. All at once came the delighted sounds of animals enjoying a tasty meal.

"So good," they murmured.

"Incredible," they exclaimed.

"It's nature's jelly bean," said a delighted Cotton-tail.

"Problem is the dried fruit's at the center of the market," said Barnabas, interrupting their groans of delight. "Surrounded by all the farmers."

The rabbits imagined a mob of the angriest, toughest farmers they'd ever seen, and that included the Old Mr. McGregor.

"But even if we take care of them, we gotta get past the toughest one of all – the dried fruit vendor herself," said Tom Kitten. "Sara Nakamoto."

The crew described a mean-faced, twelve-year-old girl. Standing at her stall, she would snatch a dried apricot from the hands of a customer, and with a glare say, "One sample per customer," without a second thought.

"Best peripheral vision in the game." Tom Kitten shook his head.

The rabbits stared wide-eyed in shock as the gang continued to explain the dangers of the mission ahead.

"Never leaves her post," stated Tom Kitten. "No matter what."

"But Sara Nakamoto has one Achilles heel," said Barnabas.

"Is it her Achilles heel?" Benjamin wondered.

"No, her actual Achilles heel is like a steel rod.

I knew a squirrel who tried to bite it once," Tom Kitten explained. "Her Achilles heel is actually the son of the cheesemonger across the aisle – Simon Pemberly."

The rabbits recalled the look of love that had passed between Bea and Thomas in the early days of their romance. They pictured now the same sickly look as Sara Nakamoto clapped eyes on the young Simon Pemberly while he leaned on his giant tower of cheese wheels and almost caused them to topple off the table. It was true teenage love.

"We create *total chaos*, getting all the farmers to leave their stands and chase us," said Barnabas.

"Then we knock Simon to the ground – *boom-skada-boom* – young Miss Nakamoto rushes over in romantic concern," jumped in Mittens.

"And that's when we strike," pressed Barnabas.

"How do we get the fruit out of there?" Peter asked.

"The tailor always comes to the market just before it closes to buy his weekly sausage," said Tom Kitten. "We haul it onto his truck and he drives it right back here for us. *Bag-a-boo smack-a-doo*."

Barnabas and his gang seemed very pleased with their plan but Peter and his family still had a few questions . . .

"How do we get away?" asked Cotton-tail.

Barnabas smiled. "That's the best part," he said. "We don't. We run into the petting zoo and blend in with the other animals."

It seemed as though Barnabas had thought of everything.

"But we're gonna need a bigger crew," he said. "Hoping you can help with that."

"We're gonna need a pickpocket," said Mittens.

The rabbits pictured their friends back at home and one animal immediately came to mind . . . Tommy Brock.

"How about a lazy badger who's scared of the rain?" suggested Peter.

"Some muscle," continued Samuel Whiskers.

"How about a well-dressed pig who likes to dance when no one's watching?" said Cotton-tail.

"An electronics expert," stated Mittens.

"How about a cranky hedgehog who likes to sleep in the buff?" replied Mopsy in excitement.

"We don't need to go through all this," said Peter confidently. "We'll find them."

And, just like that, the mission was on.

Chapter Seventeen

Outside the McGregor Manor, Thomas loaded his prized tomatoes into his Land Rover. At the same time, Bea tore up the drive in her new convertible. She jumped out of the car and strode toward her husband.

"Why'd you tell Nigel I didn't want his ideas?" she exclaimed.

"No," said Thomas. "I was just talking about how I felt you were losing your voice and compromising your – "

But Bea was too angry to hear Thomas and cut him off. "You have no right to speak for me," she declared angrily. "Nigel said he was going to reduce the run of the second book because it was too *niche*."

"It's *nitch*," muttered Thomas unhelpfully.

"No, it's *niche*," stormed Bea.

The couple continued to argue over the English language. And like most arguments between adults, they said the same silly things over and over without listening to each other.

"It is too pronounced *nitch*. It's anglicized. Like us," Thomas argued.

"It's *niche*, from the Latin. Let's not forget where we came from. And I'm sure you haven't filled up the truck either, because I saw your work gloves in the kitchen," Bea retorted.

"I *did* fill the truck – achoo! It's *nitch* and my family's not from *Latin*, we're from Antwerp!"

The fight continued. And again, like most arguments between adults, they weren't arguing about what they were really arguing about . . .

"Brussels is the capital of Belgium. Has been, is, and will continue to be!"

"What if Antwerp makes a play for it? Capitals have moved before, and will move again! Kyoto, Japan, eighteen sixty-nine. Where are those moving trucks going – Tokyo!"

After a lot of tense and not relevant words, Bea eventually got to the point.

"I'm finally having some success and I'm determined to hold on to it," she sniffed. "So please just support me and don't go behind my back, OK?"

"You're right," Thomas agreed. "I shouldn't have done that. But this isn't you, Bea. You paint elegant stories about the rabbits and our home and our family."

"I *am* painting our family . . . the best-*selling* version of our family," she pressed.

"OK, I'm sorry," Thomas backed down. "But to be honest, that's not my version of our family."

Moments later Bea walked into her cottage. There on the table in the hall was a parcel from Nigel Basil-Jones. Bea opened the box to reveal the wacky stuffed-animal versions of her beloved family. There was Benjamin as a spaceman, Cotton-tail dressed as a cowgirl, Flopsy a luau dancer in a Hawaiian skirt, and Mopsy dressed in a leotard, tutu, and ballet shoes. And Peter – well, he was clearly meant to be the bad seed, for his stuffed toy was a robber wearing a ski mask. On his back was a string. Bea pulled the string.

"I'm so baaaaaad. No school for me," the toy Peter rang out.

Bea pulled it again.

"I'm a baaaaad rabbit. Put up yer dukes!"

Bea gasped in horror. "Oh my god."

She tossed the stuffed toys back into the box as quickly as she could, but as she went to close the box, the muffled voice of another animal called out. Bea rooted around to find the source of the voice. It was Mrs. Tiggy-winkle dressed as a chef.

"I'm Mrs. Tiggy-winkle! What's cooking, y'all?"

"This is awful," cried Bea as she looked around

112

the house. Suddenly it dawned on her that her family wasn't by her side, as it usually was. "Where are my babies, anyway?"

Because, of course, Bea still didn't know that her babies were in Gloucester. Or that they were about to pull off the *greatest farmers' market heist in history*. Never mind that it was also the first. Peter had always been a trailblazer, for better or worse. And he was determined this mission was going to be for the better.

Later that day, the farmers' market was in full swing. Couples strolled lazily through the stalls, examining the different goods for sale, while shoppers merrily filled their bags with fresh produce.

Meanwhile, children's excited laughter could be heard as they rode ponies inside Piperson's Petting Zoo, while a folk band entertained the crowd.

Behind each stall stood the farmers, looking as menacing as ever. Or so the rabbits thought! In the very center of the market stood Sara Nakamoto, sneaking glances across at Simon Pemberly, with his twelve-foot tower of cheese wheels, in between swift dried-fruit sales.

The tailor's truck snaked its way through the busy streets toward this merriment. The gang was also in position. They were all waiting in an alley at the edge of the market. If a human had thought to look down the alley, they would have been in for a bit of a shock, for the rabbits, cats, and rat had been joined by some more friends. Tommy Brock, Pigling Bland, Mrs. Tiggy-winkle, Jemima Puddle-duck, Felix D'eer, and Jeremy Fisher all stood watching the market unfold.

"That's a lot of farmers," squeaked Mrs. Tiggy-winkle.

"And a lot of lavender body wash," snorted Pigling Bland.

"How did we get here?" asked a confused Tommy Brock.

"I know," agreed Jemima. "We're in over our heads."

"No, I mean literally," Tommy Brock continued. "I was napping in a tree, someone called me, I remember moving fast over land . . ."

Benjamin could see this line of conversation wasn't going to go anywhere anytime soon.

"Peter," he suggested. "May I have a quick word?"

Peter nodded and he and his sisters followed Benjamin to one side of the alley. Benjamin squared his shoulders and looked his cousin directly in the eye.

"As provisional leader of this family, I have to say . . . stealing from McGregor was one thing, but we don't know these people. They didn't do anything to us."

But Peter was not in the mood to listen to reason.

"Who paved over the city?" he asked. "Rabbits? Pigs? Mouses? No. Farmers."

"Did they?" asked Flopsy, sounding shocked.

"Don't they just plant stuff?" questioned Mopsy.

"It doesn't matter," Peter went on. "We were here first."

"Were we?" said Flopsy.

"Kind of a free-for-all back then, wasn't it?" suggested Mopsy.

Peter shook his head. "So what? It's ours for the taking."

"Yeah, but why take it?" pointed out Benjamin.

"To eat!" Peter exclaimed.

"Really?" huffed Benjamin. "It's about that?"

By now Peter had had enough. "You think I'm doing this because I was called 'bad' for so long I sought comfort in the arms of a thief and that criminality might actually be my birthright and a way to get love from my father?"

As Peter spoke, his voice rose higher and higher, the more frustrated he became. Flopsy decided it was a good time to point this out.

"Your voice," she said simply.

"Is it high again?" asked Peter. "It's high again."

Cotton-tail gave him a firm smack.

"I miss Dad so much," Peter barked in a very low, deep voice. It still wasn't right.

Cotton-tail smacked him again.

"I didn't ask you to come and find me," he said softly, his voice now back to normal. "If you want to run back to Bea and McGregor and let them control your lives, have it your way. The train station's right over there."

"So *that's* how we got here." Tommy Brock smiled, pleased to have solved the mystery.

"This is who I am," Peter said to his family as Barnabas smiled proudly and put an arm round his shoulders. "I'm doing this. Are you with me?"

The animals nodded. They were in. There was never any doubt when it came to Peter.

Chapter Eighteen

At that moment, the tailor's van pulled up outside the market.

"It's time." Samuel Whiskers nodded.

Peter and Barnabas charged from their hiding place with the other animals in hot pursuit. They all ran into the marketplace, laying siege to anyone and anything that dared get in their way. They toppled over carts laden with blueberries and butternut squash. They played a game of catch with some juicy-looking peaches and smashed aubergines to smithereens.

Customers fled from the mayhem and vegetable gunk that seemed to be coming from every direction. Farmers, meanwhile, attempted to defend their produce with raised hoes and fists. But their efforts were in vain; it was pandemonium. The marauding animals nipped with ease between the angry humans.

Flopsy sprinted through the legs of one particularly angry-looking farmer who brought down her hoe and narrowly missed the little rabbit.

Another farmer swiped at Mopsy with his knife but she avoided the blade with a spectacular somersault. In midair she slapped the farmer across the face with an enormous radish. The farmer staggered backward into a stool that Benjamin had already moved into position. He teetered for a moment and then fell to the ground with a thud.

Meanwhile, Jemima Puddle-duck dive-bombed farmers left, right, and center, and Jeremy Fisher whacked them with his fishing rod. In the chaos, his rod caught a shopper.

"No civilians!" Jemima squawked.

"He was wearing overalls!" Jeremy retorted.

Just then, a bowling ball took out another farmer. It was Mrs. Tiggy-winkle. The farmer looked at the hedgehog and recognition dawned on his face.

"Is that the hedgehog from the billboard?" he asked.

Mrs. Tiggy-winkle paused and struck the pose from the billboard and continued to roll on through the market.

Over by the apple stall, Pigling Bland was adeptly dancing and dodging the fruit being hurled at him by an enraged farmer. He blocked one with his hoof and kicked it back at the farmer as he performed a very agile cartwheel for such a large pig that enjoyed his food. The apple hit the farmer squarely between the eyes.

"This little piggy went to market," he smirked.

Outside the market hall, Samuel Whiskers, Tom Kitten, and Mittens waited for the tailor to get out of his truck. Just as he was about to shut the doors, the gang slipped through the gap to wait.

With the market in utter chaos and the farmers distracted, there were only Sara Nakamoto and Simon Pemberly left. Tommy Brock snagged a rope from one of the tents and looped it over Felix D'eer's antlers. He crept over to Sara Nakamoto's stand and hooked the other end of the rope on to the back end of her dried-fruit cart.

"Now!" shouted Barnabas.

Together, Barnabas and Peter dashed under legs and hurtled over boxes as they raced toward Simon's cheese tower that stood directly ahead. Suddenly, and in perfect harmony, the rabbits leaped into the air and kicked the tower. WHA-BAM! It toppled over and squashed Simon underneath.

"Siiiiiiiiimonnnn!" called Sara Nakamoto. She rushed to her crush's side.

Peter and Barnabas looked at each other in triumph. *We did it!* But then they noticed an enormous wheel of cheese making its way toward them . . . and it was picking up speed.

Peter looked at the cheese and his face suddenly dropped in horror! *It couldn't be? But it was.* There in its path and about to be flattened by a three-hundred-pound cheese wheel was none other than Thomas McGregor himself. McGregor, who was attempting to sell his prized tomatoes, watched dumbstruck as the giant cheese wheel raced toward his precious tomato stall. He looked up and his eyes locked with Peter's.

"Peter?" he said in confusion.

Peter, in shock, tried to stop the cheese but he was too late. It smashed into Thomas and his tomato stall. It knocked McGregor to the ground and crushed almost every box of tomatoes.

A hurt expression crossed Thomas's face. What had Peter just done?

But there was no time to ponder the enormity of the calamity that had just occurred. At that moment, Tommy Brock smacked Felix D'eer on the rear. The big deer took off toward the entrance and the tailor's truck, dragging the dried-fruit cart behind him.

"Let's go, son," said Barnabas, and raced after the runaway deer.

Almost in slow motion, Peter looked from Barnabas to Thomas and back to Barnabas before

120

he, too, hopped after the stag. Part one of the mission was complete.

Outside the market, it was time to execute the next part of the heist. Mittens and Tom Kitten opened the rear doors as Felix ran past. Samuel Whiskers scampered from the truck and jumped into the path of a passing car.

The driver screeched to a halt. Its daytime lights shone directly into the eyes of Felix D'eer.

"Heeeeeeeaaaaadliiiiights," murmured Felix, entranced.

His sudden stop caused the dried-fruit cart to crash into the bumper of the truck and bins of fruit slid out and onto the back of the truck. The kittens slammed the doors shut.

"*Cracka-jacka*," Tom Kitten grinned.

Chapter Nineteen

Meanwhile, the other animals raced to Piperson's Petting Zoo. Samuel Whiskers unlocked the gate and they flooded into the pen with the rest of the petting animals.

Unseen, Samuel Whiskers closed the gate. He was just in time, for it wasn't long before a group of angry farmers arrived, looking for the culprits. Not finding any, they headed back to what was left of their stalls.

Barnabas turned to the gang. "Head for the truck one by one so you don't draw attention," he instructed.

Whiskers opened the gate and Barnabas sneaked out. He gestured for Peter to follow and they made their way to the tailor's truck. Peter tried to look back to see if Thomas was all right.

"Stay focused, son," Barnabas reminded him. "What's done is done."

With the two rabbits on their way to safety, Benjamin stepped toward the gate only to have Whiskers slam it shut in his face with a *clank*! He jammed a stick in the lock for good measure and grinned wickedly at the trapped animals in the petting pen.

"Nice knowin' ya." He smirked before dashing off to join the truck.

"Hey, what are you doing?" called Benjamin.

Samuel Whiskers burst through the open truck doors just as it zoomed into life and began to pull away.

"Where is everyone?" asked Peter.

Silence filled the truck as Peter raced to the window. His face aghast, he watched his family and friends being stuffed into cages and shoved into Piperson's van. The petting zoo was closed for the day.

"No!" he shouted.

At that moment, Thomas McGregor emerged from the market, too. His anger turned to concern when he saw the animals trapped in the van.

"What are you doing?" he yelled at the petting zoo workers. "Let them go!"

In the tailor's van, Peter was yelling the same thing. "Let them go! What are they doing?"

Peter tried to grab the door handle but was held back by Barnabas.

"Don't get yourself caught, too, son," he warned.

"But if you did, it would just be a bigger share for us anyways, innit?" Samuel Whiskers suggested.

Tom Kitten and Mittens laughed cruelly. Knowingly. Peter took one last look outside and locked eyes with Thomas McGregor.

"Hey! Stop!" McGregor shouted, but the tailor's van moved off down the road.

SLAM! At the same time, the pet shop van doors closed and it, too, drove off with Thomas calling after it, "Wait! Stop!"

As the truck drove back to the tailor's shop, Peter began to piece together the events of the last few hours.

"You set us up," he announced.

Tom Kitten slapped tails with Mittens and replied with a gleeful expression across his whiskers. "We didn't *not* set you up, if you catch my smell. *Bingbong.*"

"You really thought we were going to share all this with those bumpkins?" Barnabas explained. "We just needed bodies. Sweet, dumb, country bodies that don't ask questions."

Peter gasped. "That's my family. Dad was your best friend."

"And my best friend was the sugar plum fairy," snickered Samuel Whiskers.

The truth dawned on Peter. He had been set up good and proper.

"You never knew my dad," he stated.

124

"Wouldn't be caught dead in some country garden," Barnabas affirmed. "Like he was."

"Why did you do this?" asked Peter.

"No one wanted to adopt me," Barnabas continued. "I was too old."

Peter pictured a rather scruffy and sad-looking Barnabas in the cage of a pet shop, being passed over by children holding their own copies of Bea's *Peter Rabbit* book.

"Every kid in town wanted a young rabbit like the one in that book," said Barnabas.

"First book he's read in years," explained Whiskers. "And it's mostly pictures."

"So I asked around," Barnabas continued, remembering how he gave some cheese to Johnny Town-mouse in return for information on Peter. "I was just gonna use you as bait for a few fake-and-takes, but then I saw how good you were and I figured we could do something a lot bigger together."

Peter's eyes narrowed. "You lied to me."

"It's not hard to lie to someone who wants to believe," Barnabas said. "But one thing is true – we're a great team. That's why you're in this truck with us instead of in a cage with them."

Tears filled Peter's eyes as anger welled up inside his furry body.

"This is where you belong, Peter," said Barnabas. "We're your family now."

"No," blurted Peter angrily. "My family's in trouble and I'm going to save them."

With that, the hero of our story threw himself at the truck door. KA-KLANG! It flew open and he tumbled out onto the street as the truck sped off down the road. Peter lay sprawled across the pavement. He lifted his head in time to see Barnabas looking back from the open door of the truck.

"Want us to take care of him?" asked Mittens from behind.

"Nah. Leave him," Barnabas replied. He watched as Peter darted out of the way of a passing car and ran off down the street. "He's a good kid, or he would have seen this coming."

Chapter Twenty

The dim lights in the petting zoo truck added to the doom and gloom that was already keenly felt by the animals stacked in cages high up to the ceiling.

"Did Peter set us up?" asked Cotton-tail quietly.

Flopsy jumped to her brother's defense. "No, he wouldn't do that."

"He's not here, is he?" Benjamin pointed out.

A scared silence filled the air.

They didn't know that at that very moment, Peter was doing his utmost to reach them. He was sprinting down the road as fast as his legs would carry him when a convertible sped past. The driver glanced back in confusion. *Was that Peter?* thought Bea, but she didn't have time to stop and find out.

Peter ran all the way to Piperson's Pets and spotted the van parked outside. As Peter approached the store, the door opened and out walked a large man carrying a cage. Inside was a frightened pink pig. It was Pigling Bland.

Peter hid behind a parked car and continued to watch in horror as his friends came out one by one. A mother and her daughter were carrying Mrs. Tiggy-winkle. And right behind them came a family with a sad-looking Benjamin. His cage was quickly loaded into the car and the family drove away.

Peter's eyes settled on a sign above the door. **BUY THE ANIMALS FROM PETER RABBIT!** He bounded to the shop and peered in through the window. All the cages were empty and the workers were busy sweeping up. A large display of *Peter Rabbit* books was in the center of the now empty store.

They're gone? Peter thought as his body sagged. What had he done? His heart felt like it had been broken as he stared at his own sorry reflection in the window.

"Peter?" a familiar voice called out suddenly.

Peter turned around, and there was Thomas McGregor.

"Was that Benjamin? Where are the others?" Thomas continued. "What have you done?"

Peter looked up at the banner above the shop front again and Thomas's eyes followed. He began to piece it all together.

"I can't believe you," McGregor moaned. "I mean, I *can* believe you. It's what you do – create mayhem."

And with that, he headed into the shop with a chastened Peter Rabbit following behind.

Across the city, in a packed conference room, a large screen showed an animated video of the rabbits playing ukuleles and singing a rather lame song.

> *"Because together we can do anything!*
> *Rely on the power of one!*
> *The power of one!"*

Toward the end of the song, Benjamin, who was barely recognizable as Benjamin, strutted across the screen and finished his solo line in a bass voice.

"The power of one!"

Then the lights went up to reveal Nigel Basil-Jones and his executives who were giving the presentation to Bea. They were all applauding and hooting loudly.

"Amazing! So cute!" they chorused.

"That's just one idea the team came up with for a possible movie version," an executive exclaimed.

Bea sat there in shock.

"They don't really look or act like my rabbits," she said politely.

"We'll totally transfer all your brainwork onto it," another executive assured her. 'The director is *very* collaborative. He's Norwegian."

At this point Nigel piped up with his usual enthusiasm. "We couldn't be more excited, Bea," he cried. "Your latest changes have got us almost to the finish line."

There was an echo of agreement from the others in the room.

"But I think some of your pages are missing," another executive offered. "The end is just the rabbits making tea as Peter apologizes."

"That's right," said Bea. "That's what they do. They learn from their mistakes."

The room filled with groans and Bea looked around her, crestfallen.

"I think what we're trying to say is," said Nigel pleasantly, "the ending is really important. It's the only thing readers remember."

There were nods from every corner of the room as a researcher via video link began to speak. "The first eighty percent can be absolute drivel, but if the final chapter is jam-packed with exciting action and emotion? *Bestseller.*"

Bea wanted to please these publishing folks. After all, they knew about books.

"OK, OK," she said. "What if . . . one of them goes

to town to get a birthday gift —"

"And she gets kidnapped!" an executive exclaimed.

"They should all get kidnapped," another suggested. "There can be a rescue mission, exotic locations, all over the country, even *outside* the country."

Bea felt overwhelmed as they continued to talk about wild car chases in Italy, getting revenge on gangs of bad guys, motorcycles, boats, and rabbits riding off into a sunset.

"The sunset should be pink, though, as testing tells us that's the color of hope and the future," an executive added while everyone else cheered.

"This is it, Bea!" said Nigel. "Everything you've ever wanted."

But was it?

Chapter Twenty-one

Back inside the pet shop, McGregor was talking to the pet shop worker (while Peter hid, watched, and waited).

"Sorry, stretch," said the owner. "Can't tell you who took 'em. Private information. Against the law to give it out."

"This is a pet shop. Not an adoption agency. I *demand* you give me that list this very instant," Thomas said in exasperation.

"Oh, you demand, do you? I didn't realize the gravity. Jonno! Did you hear? He demands!"

Thomas's face began to turn pink as the two shop workers exchanged jokes at his expense. Suddenly, Jonno recognized McGregor from the market.

"Oy, you're that beanpole from the market with the tomatoes. They were bangin'."

Thomas smiled, quickly becoming distracted by the praise heaped upon his precious tomatoes. "Why, thank you," he said. "I cross-germinated a Brandywine with a San Marzano, but my real trick is massaging the buds till just before they flower and – "

Taking the opportunity at hand, Peter broke away from his hiding spot and snatched the list unexpectantly from the store worker's hands. Then he and McGregor made a dash for the door.

Inside the car, the pair looked at the list.

"OK, first stop, almond milk, cashew cheese, and walnut butter. This is not the list but the man clearly gets his protein from nuts."

Peter and McGregor glanced at one another and headed back to the store.

THWUMP! The shopkeeper looked up to see McGregor's last box of tomatoes on the counter.

"The tomatoes for the list," McGregor said through gritted teeth.

Back inside McGregor's Land Rover, and with the real list this time, the pair set off to rescue the animals.

"Manchester, Inverness, the Alps – they're everywhere," muttered McGregor. "See the mess you made! You're never going to learn."

"Because you never give me a chance," Peter replied. "All you do is tell me how bad I am."

"Then stop giving me reasons to," Thomas retorted. "Did you just talk?"

Peter waved a paw. "Yes, no, could be your imagination."

Suddenly, the Land Rover lurched to a stop. McGregor looked at the fuel gauge. It was empty. "Aagh!"

Thomas and Peter had no choice but to get out and push the Land Rover down the street. As they inched slowly toward their destination, Peter was determined to make his point.

"No matter what I do, you always assume the worst," he grumbled.

But Thomas wasn't about to accept he was to blame. "You just destroyed an entire farmers' market and you got your family taken!" he huffed, the effort of pushing the car being mainly on him. "If that's not the worst, what is?"

"Why are you even helping me?" asked Peter.

Thomas paused for a moment. "I don't know," he sighed. "I saw you all get caught and I just had to come. Wasn't a choice."

The pair continued to push the car in uncomfortable silence for a moment. Peter jumped up against the bumper again and again. After all there was little else he could do from his height.

After a moment, he stopped. "I don't think I'm actually propelling this thing in any real way."

McGregor put his whole back into it in response.

"I'm sorry I wrecked your tomatoes," continued Peter. "That wasn't supposed to happen."

McGregor turned to look at Peter. "What *was* supposed to happen?"

Peter returned Thomas's gaze sheepishly. "I met someone who made me feel like not everything I did was wrong. Who actually accepted me," he said in a pained voice. "But it was all a lie. He used me to rob the market. I'm so stupid."

McGregor looked across at the little rabbit's sunken shoulders.

"You're not stupid," he said gently. "You're just a kid. Who makes mistakes. A *lot* of mistakes."

"It's one thing I'm really good at," said Peter dejectedly.

"And you're not the bad seed," McGregor continued. "I'm sorry I called you that . . . I know sometimes I'm too hard on you. I lost my father when I was very young, too. I don't really know how to be one."

"To me?" Peter asked in astonishment.

A look of realization crossed McGregor's face. It was as if he finally understood what Bea had always said about her beloved children . . . her rabbits.

"Yeah, to you," he replied. "And the others. That's why I'm here, I guess. It's what a dad does."

"I didn't think I'd have a dad again," said Peter.

"I didn't realize I already was one," said McGregor. "But you have to tell me if you can talk. This is ridiculous!"

Peter shrugged and smiled.

Chapter Twenty-two

Later that same day, Bea was still stuck inside the conference room at Nigel Basil-Jones's office. It was the merchandising part of the presentation and the table was covered in Peter Rabbit merchandise.

One executive grinned with glee as she told Bea, "It's still early, but a leading cold-cut company wants to stamp your little dudes on every slice of their bologna!"

"One of my characters is actually a pig, so . . . ," said Bea hesitantly.

"Perfect!" Nigel cut in. "It's a rare treat to see an artist with a mind for business."

Suddenly, the door crashed open and in tumbled Peter and Thomas.

"So sorry to interrupt," said Thomas. Then he turned to his wife. "Bea, may I have a word?"

"Thomas?" said Bea.

"You brought Peter! Terrific!" said Nigel gleefully, and snatched up the unsuspecting rabbit. "Now we can show everyone what Peter would look like in zero gravity."

Nigel grabbed an empty water jug from the table and stuffed it on the head of a terrified Peter.

"Just imagine the others floating next to him." Then, in his best Darth Vader voice he began to act out the scene in space. "Come on, Flopso! We've gotta get back to the rocket ship! Copy!"

Bea was aghast. "Nigel! Stop it!" she shouted as she watched her beloved rabbit in distress. Quickly, she grabbed Peter and took off his 'helmet.' He gasped for air before delivering a little kick to Nigel's ribs.

"You OK, sweetie?" she asked him.

"Bea, the other rabbits were taken," Thomas interrupted.

"What?" she asked.

"They were put in a pet shop and sold off," McGregor continued. "Also the duck, the pig, the hedgehog, and I think . . . the badger?"

Peter nodded.

"Yes, the badger," confirmed Thomas. "I need your car to go and get them."

"Oh my god," cried Bea. "How did this happen?"

"Because we weren't around," said Thomas seriously. "I just need your car, I don't mean to interrupt."

Bea looked around at the merchandise on the table. It dawned on her that all this couldn't be further from her family if she tried.

"What have I done?" she said.

"Written eighty percent of a bestseller," Nigel Basil-Jones responded. "Just get some more rabbits. Get a million more with the money you're about to make."

But Bea wasn't listening anymore. She turned to Peter and rested her forehead on his. "I'm so sorry." Then Bea turned to face her publisher. "I'm sorry I led you all on, but I can't do this," she said. "This isn't my world."

"Not your world?" barked Nigel. "Look around! All we need is for you to write that ending!"

But Bea shook her head. "There's no skiing or parachuting or boat chases in my world. And my rabbits don't go to space."

Nigel was seething. "Bea, what are you doing?" he breathed. "Do you know how much I put into this?"

"I need to go and get my family," said Bea as she and Peter joined McGregor at the door. "Goodbye, Nigel."

Bea and Thomas took each other's hands and smiled as they heard Nigel call from the conference room, "I want my car back!"

"Forgot to top up the truck, eh?" Bea smiled at Thomas.

Bea, Thomas, and Peter had a lot to catch up on as they hopped into the convertible. Peter was in the middle at the back, leaning forward between the happy couple.

"Take a left at the church," he instructed.

"OK," agreed Bea. Then she looked across to McGregor. "Did he just talk?"

Thomas shrugged. "Don't know. Best not to overthink it."

And so, reunited, they tore off down the street to rescue the rest of their family.

Chapter Twenty-three

They arrived at the first house on the list. Bea and Peter waited in the car, while a woman happily handed back Jemima Puddle-duck to McGregor.

Next stop was the science classroom of a school. They just managed to rescue Jeremy Fisher in time before he was dissected in the name of science.

But not everyone was quite so willing to part with their new pets. A boatman was onboard his boat. A caged Benjamin sat beside a pot of boiling water while the man chopped vegetables. He snarled and shook his head as Bea and Thomas pleaded with him to release Benjamin.

"Promised the missus stew," he barked.

This quest set the heroes off on a final rescue mission, jam-packed with lots of action, chases, exotic locations, and different vehicles – the likes of which Bea insisted never happened in her world.

As the family chased down the angry boatman in their own speedboat, Bea could hardly believe what was happening. She watched from the helm as McGregor threw a grappling hook with style. It fastened securely to the stern of the boatman's vessel.

Peter tightrope-walked swiftly across the rope to the boat ahead and released Benjamin from his cage. But as they celebrated his freedom, the boatman jammed an oar into the helm and bore down on Peter and Benjamin with his vegetable knife. He cut the rope connecting the two boats. The rabbits were trapped. There was no way out.

Without looking back, Peter and Benjamin jumped off the boat . . . right into a waiting outboard motor dinghy. Benjamin pulled the start just like a sailor that he'd always dreamed of being, and captained the boat away from the very angry, and probably very hungry, boatman.

"You OK?" asked Peter a moment later.

"Not with you," snapped Benjamin.

"I deserve that," said Peter solemnly.

Mopsy's rescue was next. An aeroplane was flying in midair with its doors wide open. McGregor was dressed in parachuting gear, holding tightly to Mopsy as a shocked little girl inside the plane clutched her empty pet cage. At that moment, Peter jumped onto McGregor's back and they leaped to freedom.

Bea and the other animals sped along the road underneath the parachute. McGregor landed perfectly in the car and – ZWOOSH – he released the parachute, which caught in the antlers of Felix D'eer, taking him high into the sky.

Next up was a grand and luxurious mansion. Bea and the rabbits rushed inside to find Cotton-tail on a pile of silk cushions. She was gorging herself on jelly beans.

"I don't want to go!" she cried.

But the rabbits dragged her outside, while she tried to hold on to the mansion and the promise of infinite jelly beans. They bundled her into the convertible and it sped off.

Soon, the family found themselves in the Italian Alps, attempting to rescue Tommy Brock. First, though, they stopped for gas.

"This is how you fill up the car." Bea winked at her husband.

Bea and McGregor deftly skied down the snowy slopes as they weaved through trees and chased an Italian skier clutching the badger. Peter and Benjamin were perched on the front of the skis, using them like snowboards. They snatched the frightened badger triumphantly from the skier's grasp. Victory!

While the rabbits, Bea, and Thomas dashed around the world and rescued their family, Barnabas and his gang had uncovered something rather astonishing.

Back inside the tailor's shop, they opened the bins. Every single one of them was empty. Barnabas could not believe it!

"You shoulda let me take care of him," said Samuel Whiskers unhelpfully.

And perhaps Samuel Whiskers had been right, for at that very moment Bea's convertible was cruising away from a farmhouse deep in the country. A sign read, **NAKAMOTO FAMILY FARMS**.

Sara Nakamoto and Simon Pemberly made their way outside and found all the full bins of dried fruit on their porch.

Chapter Twenty-four

Meanwhile, the family continued their rescue mission. Inside a butcher's shop, Peter breathed on the door of a large walk-in refrigerator. The others watched in awe as he drew an X on the door before taking a flying leap. It opened instantly to reveal a freezing Pigling Bland, his teeth chattering.

Suddenly, the rabbits heard a noise. They turned just in time to see an angry butcher in an apron. The animals made a dash for the car. As soon as they were safe, the group sped away with the butcher chasing after them on his motorbike.

Bea expertly navigated the streets and alleys, even careering down a flight of stairs at one point, but she had met her match. The butcher could not be shaken. As the car reached the docks, the butcher's motorbike pulled up alongside the convertible. No one knew what was going to happen next but Mrs. Tiggy-winkle didn't want to wait to find out.

Without hesitation, she leaped on to the butcher's face. This surprise act caused the butcher to lose control of the bike. As it crashed, he flew off the dock and into the water below. Mrs. Tiggy-winkle jumped back into the car and looked at her friends.

"And that's why I'm on the billboard," she said smugly. The animals and Bea and Thomas couldn't help but agree.

But as Bea and McGregor turned their attention back to the road, their faces fell. Straight ahead was a small building site and there was no way to avoid it. *CRUNCH!* The car crashed into the building and continued on its way. It sent wood and splinters everywhere, and revealed a man sitting on a now exposed toilet reading the newspaper. A metal sign sailed through the air and landed on Flopsy's lap. It read, **LAVATORY**.

"That's what it means?" she gasped sadly.

Mopsy nodded guiltily.

"A place to read newspapers?" Flopsy continued.

Mopsy smiled at her sister and said, "There's no one in the world I'd rather be confused with than you, Flops."

"Same here, Mops," Flopsy replied and the two sisters nuzzled each other.

Later the same day, Peter and the rabbits were back in a Gloucester alley and he was holding a sweet potato.

"Be right back," he said to his sisters and Benjamin.

Peter entered the kitchen of a restaurant and carefully placed the sweet potato on top of a huge pile of the same vegetable. The cook looked at the rabbit in confusion but didn't stop him as Peter inched from the room.

Peter returned to the alley to find his family had disappeared. He could see Bea and Thomas in the convertible a little way down the alley with the other animals but no rabbits.

"Well, well, well," said a voice. Peter turned to see Barnabas. "Looks like you're a goody-goody after all, kid."

Barnabas, Whiskers, Tom Kitten, and Mittens had grabbed Peter's rabbit family. They looked scared out of their minds.

"Let them go," said Peter.

"Where's our loot, rabbit?" Mittens replied.

"Where it belongs," said Peter.

"Say goodbye to your family then," seethed Barnabas.

Peter knew he had to keep his family from coming to any harm. "I'm the one you want. Take me and I'll show you," he insisted.

"Wow," laughed Barnabas. "Acting all tough, in charge. You did learn from me."

147

Barnabas nodded to Tom Kitten, who grabbed Peter as Mittens and Whiskers let the triplets and Benjamin go. The gang hauled Peter away.

"Peter!" cried Benjamin.

"It'll be all right," he replied. "Just go."

The triplets turned to race toward Bea's car but it had vanished. Peter was being marched away by Barnabas and his crew when suddenly the animals heard the revving of an engine. Bea zoomed down the alley from the opposite direction. The gang let go of Peter and scattered at the sight of the angry woman driving like a crazy person down a narrow alley.

McGregor opened the car door and Peter quickly hopped inside. At the same time, Tommy Brock and Pigling Bland grabbed Benjamin and the triplets, and Bea tore out of the alley and back onto the main road.

After a moment's stunned silence, Benjamin gently asked Peter, "You OK?"

"Of course," said Peter. "I knew he'd save me."

"How?" asked Flopsy.

"It's what dads do," smiled Peter bravely.

Bea reached over and took Thomas's hand. "Let's go home."

Chapter Twenty-five

The family began the long journey back to their countryside home, with sirens following them as Nigel had reported the car stolen.

"You were right," Thomas said. "I should have just supported you. I think I was worried the book would take you away from me, from our life, from the family I wanted us to have. I'm sorry."

"No, *I'm* sorry," she insisted. "I was chasing something for all the wrong reasons."

In the backseat, Peter was also apologizing.

"I'm sorry," he said. "I never should've put you in danger. I got caught up worrying about who everyone thought I was, instead of who I really am. Which is your brother." He touched foreheads with his sisters and then Benjamin. "And your cousin," Peter continued. "Who continues to not listen to you but promises to really, really try."

"You are who you are. But I love ya," Benjamin smiled, touching foreheads with Peter.

Pigling Bland began to nudge his way toward the rabbits. He wanted to touch foreheads, too, but Benjamin put his arms out to stop the pig's advances.

"Sorry. Family only."

"No, no," said Peter kindly. "I let everyone down." He rested his head on Pigling's and sniffed. "Is that lavender?"

Meanwhile, up front, Bea was still apologizing to Thomas.

"I lost sight of what was important," she pressed. "My family."

"Families come in all shapes and sizes," Thomas replied. "I see that now."

Bea couldn't help but laugh at these words. "Nigel wanted me to end my book with those exact words. I mean, the sentiment's right, but how lame!"

Thomas pretended to laugh along. "Yeah, totally, so lame!"

As the pink sunset settled over the car, the couple reached back to pet Peter and the others. Their family. They were going home.

The next morning, back in Windermere, JW Rooster II was sleeping soundly as the sun rose on a new day. His teenagers watched the big ball of fire lift high into the sky without their help.

But they cried out anyway. "Cock-a-doodle doo!"

At that moment, the sprinklers came on.

"Wait a second," crowed JW Rooster III. "Cock-a-doodle doo!"

Again, the sprinklers came on. The teenager looked at his brothers with wide eyes.

"Dad, wake up!" he cried. "Watch!"

All together the teenage roosters shouted "Cock-a-doodle doo!"

The sprinklers came on again. JW Rooster II sat up. He was amazed.

"You made the magical water fountains erupt," he squawked delightedly. "Wetting the earth, so it wouldn't burn from the giant ball of fire." He leaped to his feet. "It's not a sham! We *do* matter! We *do* have purpose! Cock-a-doodle-doo!"

The roosters all crowed together and watched as the sprinklers went off yet again.

"We're back, baby!" cried JW Rooster II as he fluttered into the air only to plummet back to the ground with a THWUMP. "But we still can't fly," he winced.

And so they all lived happily ever after. As time went by, the welcome cries of a baby could be heard through the windows of the McGregor toyshop.

McGregor seemed to be demonstrating the

latest toy doll that had arrived in the store.

"You just take the dummy out and . . ." But McGregor wasn't talking about the doll anymore. Bea and McGregor had had a child of their own. And the rabbits took to her like a real sister. The baby laughed from her cradle as her parents looked down at the happy scene before them. Peter, Benjamin, Flopsy, Mopsy, and Cotton-tail were crowding round the cradle, lovingly playing with their little sister. In doing so, her green swaddle became untucked.

Quickly, the laughter turned to bickering as the rabbits fought over who could re-swaddle her.

"No!" said Benjamin in a forceful voice that put an end to the squabbling. "It's under, fold, tuck."

He did it perfectly. At last, Benjamin had taken charge. Flopsy, too, had realized what made her different. She was the narrator of the *Peter Rabbit* stories.

"Another great story, Flopsy," said Peter. "What are you going to name it?"

Flopsy nodded over to where Bea stood with Thomas and the baby.

"She already did."

Flopsy pointed to a second Peter Rabbit book on sale in the shop – *Peter Rabbit 2*.

THE END

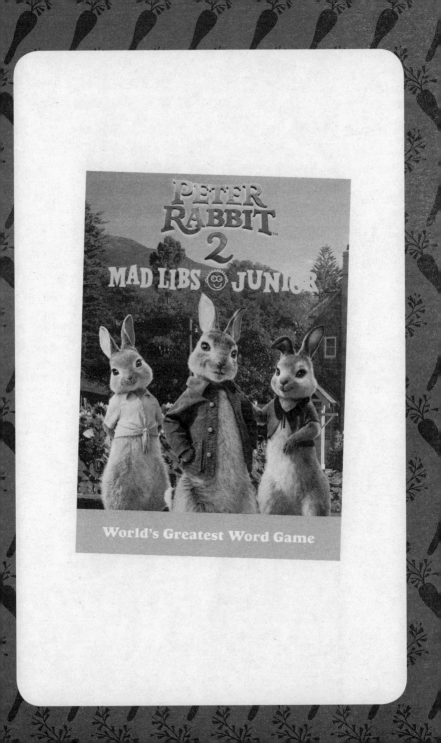

FREDERICK WARNE
An Imprint of Penguin Random House LLC, New York

First published 2020
001

Screen story and screenplay by Will Gluck and Patrick Burleigh © 2020 Columbia Pictures Industries, Inc. All Rights Reserved.

This chapter book, written by Mandy Archer
© Frederick Warne & Co. Ltd, 2020

PETER RABBIT and all associated characters ™ & © Frederick Warne & Co. Ltd, 2020. All Rights Reserved.

PETER RABBIT™ 2, the Movie © 2020 Columbia Pictures Industries, Inc. All Rights Reserved.
Images from the film PETER RABBIT™ 2, the Movie © 2020 CTMG. All Rights Reserved.

Printed in Great Britain

ISBN: 978-0-241-41530-6

BASED ON THE
MAJOR NEW MOVIE